The Centenary Chronicles

Tales of American Women

Her Last Full Measure

Written by Gail Combs Oglesby

For more information:

www.gailoglesby.wordpress.com

Interior book design and cover design

by White Rabbit Arts

at The Historical Fiction Company

ISBN 979-8-9885242-4-3 (paperback)

ISBN 979-8-9885242-5-0 (eBook)

Dedication

This book is dedicated to my Great-Great-Great Grandfather Shubal Dutton buried in Andersonville in grave 11753. He gave his life on behalf of the Union cause during the Civil War. It is his life and history that served as the inspiration for this story. While we are quick to recognize the sacrifices of those lost in war, which we should, we forget the trials of the women and children left behind in an era where there were few social systems to help them. Some of this book is an accurate retelling of those difficulties, and in other aspects a representation of the common struggles of all women of this period who lost those they loved and relied on. These women had to make their own way and in doing so they found a strength and courage they didn't know they had and didn't know they would need. I am proud to be descended from these men and women and I hope my books and my life pay homage to their memories, their dreams, and aspirations.

The Story Tellers: We are the chosen ones

In each family there is one who seems called to find the ancestors, to put flesh on their bones and make them live again, to tell the family story and to feel that somehow, they know and approve. To me, doing genealogy is not a cold gathering of facts but, instead, breathing life into all who have gone before. We are the story tellers of the tribe. All tribes have one. We have been called as it were by our genes.

Those who have gone before crying out to us: Tell our story! So, we do. In finding them, we somehow find ourselves. How many graves have I stood before and cried? I have lost count. How many times have I told the ancestors you have a wonderful family? You would be proud of us! How many times have I walked up to a grave and felt somehow there was love there for me? I cannot say.

It goes to pride in what our ancestors were able to accomplish. How they contributed to what we are today. It goes to respecting their hardships and losses, they're never giving in or giving up, their resoluteness to go on and build a life for their family. So, as a scribe called, I tell the story of my family. It is up to that one called in the next generation to answer the call and take their place in the long line of family storytellers.

Excerpt from the poem The Story Tellers attributed to

Della Joann McGinnis Johnson

Table of Contents

Chapter One – *1859*

In the distance, I could see the darkness roiling across the treetops. The swirls of clouds filled the horizon with ominous intent. The storm was coming, and it would not be long before the rain poured from the sky on our fields. The air smelled of spring, the grass, the dirt, but it also crackled with the lightning flashing in the distance making the hair on my arms stand on end. While the rain was usually a welcome sight, it would have been better to delay a few more days as there was still much more to do to prepare the fields. But we have no control over what nature, or man for that matter, brings to our doorstep and our challenge is only to find a way to use it, becoming stronger for the effort.

Many challenges have come to me and my family. Not just one, but two revolutions have touched my ancestors and by association me, one on each side of the Atlantic, in America and France. My family did not go looking for these conflicts, but the struggles found them nonetheless and it was a challenge that they did not shy away from. Instead, they took up arms to defend their property and liberty at the risk and sometimes loss, of their very lives. I am proud to call them my family and I do my best to honor them with the life I now live on our farm.

My grandfather Jean-Baptiste Beauchamp came to the American Colonies during the American Revolution to help the Continental Army of George Washington. While he was here, he met my great-uncle Benjamin Parkman, who introduced him to my grandmother Amelia. They married and returned to France which is where my mother Catherine was born as well as her sisters Marie-Elizabeth and Geneviève, and her brother Simon. But when they were just children the French Revolution began. Unrest and horrible violence in the ugliest of ways plagued the country and so they fled with little more than the clothes on their backs.

Germany provided a haven for them which was ironic given that the Hessians fought against the French and Americans during their revolution just a few years earlier but no matter, it was in the past. My mother grew up on a German farm and by the time she was seventeen she spoke English, French, German, and Dutch, with an accent she said sounded like she was from nowhere and everywhere. When she was twenty-three, she met and married my father, Arthur Streeter and they came to Oneida, New York, where I was born. My older sister Elizabeth, who we all call Bessie, and my brother James were born there as well. I am named after my mother's closest friend Millicent. My middle name is Liberty, a nod I suppose to my grandparents and great-grandparents' struggles. My mother called me Millie unless I was in trouble, and then it was Millicent Liberty without fail.

My husband Matthew usually calls me Millicent, and honestly, I much prefer it. It sounds more refined and sophisticated, although neither of those applies this warm spring day as I work in the fields my shoes covered in earth, my hair disheveled and dirty. He is a wonderful husband and a good father; strong and capable and I always feel safe when he is near. His parents were born in Germany but came to New York when he was only a child. After we married, we left New York to move west to the Michigan Territory. Land here is much more plentiful and less expensive than on the east coast and the winters are not quite so harsh, although storms in both the spring and the winter can be robust.

We have a beautiful farm here and Matthew does blacksmithing during the winter months to make extra money. We have built a sturdy and comfortable home in an area called Wales. Our farm is nearly one hundred acres, a size we never could have afforded had we stayed in New York. We do miss our families though, and Matthew is hoping his brother will come someday. We grow corn mostly, and some hay, although we also have an apple orchard and a daily garden, and we trade with our neighbors for other things we need. We do not use slaves on our farm. They have been outlawed since 1835, and even if they were legal my husband is vehemently opposed, but it always seems to be a source of constant discussion. President Pierce seems to feel that abolitionists, those who want slavery banished, will drive a wedge between the North and South where slaves are still used extensively. Some have even argued that we cannot survive as a United States with some using slaves and some so opposed but it is rhetoric so far rather than action. Secession has been talked about by the southern states since the American Revolution and states' rights versus federal laws are still a source of angst.

No matter. We manage by working together, neighbor helping neighbor, as it should be. Matthew and I are both in our thirty-sixth year and we are blessed with five beautiful children, Mariah, Rebecca, Kenneth, Cordelia, and Charles. Mariah is nearly fifteen, and the youngest, Charles, is nearly three. We have lost two babies, one born before their time and one, Richard (who we called Dickie), who died at just four from the croupe. Mariah watches the younger children while I help Matthew in the field or with milking and mucking stalls, whatever needs to be done. It is not an easy life, but it is a good life, and this land will belong to our children, hopefully for generations to come. We are not far from Lake Huron where the fishing is plentiful, and just to the south near the newly formed Port Huron, there is a thriving community of shipbuilders and lumber mills. Matthew is a skilled blacksmith, and he goes into Port Huron several times a year to do shoeing and the monies are then used for seed, tools, cloth, and staples like sugar.

"Mother," I hear Mariah's voice carry over the breeze shaking me from my thoughts, and I see her standing by the barn waving her arms frantically.

The storm still sits on the horizon as I hurry across the furrowed rows. The steam rises from the warm earth which has been freshly plowed and a smoke-like haze of fog hangs just above the ground across the field. As I get closer, I realize Mariah's dress does not make it to her ankles again. It seems as though I have just added to the hem but I will need to do so again soon.

"The calf is coming," she yelled as I drew near.

I picked up my pace. We cannot afford to lose either the calf or the cow, so it is vital that this goes smoothly. Mariah helped me through a birth last spring so she will be of great help this time.

"Mariah, get some extra water," I said as I reached the

barn.

"I have two buckets drawn mother, and a rag and I put them near the stall."

"Good girl, you remembered what to do," I said as I smiled at her. She is so smart, quick to learn new things and her memory is very good. Her sister Rebecca is not so blessed, and she is easily confused and often does not remember what she was taught just the day before. She is mostly a docile child but from time to time she can have angry tantrums which can be hard to manage, but Matthew seems to know how to calm her. She spends much of her day threshing grain or churning and the repetitive tasks seem to calm her. She can do it for hours on end, humming to herself all the while.

Mariah was right. The calf is coming, and we do our best to support the process, but the cow seems to be well in control and there is little for us to do. When the little one comes, we help to wash him up and he is healthy and already on his feet. It is a great relief, and we take a few minutes to just enjoy this miracle of new life. Soon all the children are outside, and everyone gathers around to watch the new bull as he enjoys his first taste of mother's milk. I lift Charles up to get a better view over the paddock. He is such a sweet boy.

"Cow baby," he said as he pointed to the new bull, in that

voice not quite a baby not quite a little boy.

"Yes, my lovely, that is a cow baby. He's very handsome, isn't he?" I said as I balanced him on my hip.

Matthew joins us from the field, and for a few minutes, our family laughs and enjoys the moment together before we all retreat to the house. The rain has come pounding the earth with a great force. Rain is usually a welcome visitor, but this will put us behind. The planting days on the farm wait for no one and now we must work from sunup to sundown, resting little. Once the seeds are in, we can breathe easier while nature takes over the hard work, but there are still many things to be done.

"I need to go into Port Huron in the next few days," said Matthew as he sat down to dinner.

"Can I go, Father, please?" said Mariah as she set the freshly baked bread on the table.

"Perhaps we should all go, make a day of it," I said smiling at my oldest. I know she was hoping to go without the younger children so she would be free to wander as she liked, but wandering was exactly what I did not want her to do.

"Rebecca can stay and watch the younger children," said Mariah with a whine.

"Now Mariah, you know she cannot," said Matthew

firmly.

"I can too," chimed in Rebecca.

"No, my dear, you cannot. Last time we left you with the younger children Charles almost drowned in the horse trough," I said trying not to sound dismissive.

"That was not my fault, he is a bad child," said Rebecca swatting Charles on the hand.

"Owww!" cried out Charles as he began to cry.

"Rebecca, apologize to your brother at once," I said taking him onto my lap.

"Sorry," she mumbled.

"So, it is settled. We will all go," said Matthew.

I didn't mind going to town, but it was not something I felt I needed to do as Mariah did. I know this farm life is not always to her liking and there are few others in Wales her age. Since she no longer goes to school her days are spent entirely on the farm. Taking Rebecca was a challenge as she wanted to see and touch everything, and it made it difficult to keep on task. Kenneth and Cordelia were amiable and easily followed wherever I needed to go. Maybe Matthew could take Kenneth along with him. That would leave me one less to manage. He is a good boy who obeys without a fuss.

The morning of our trip to town, Mariah was up and done with her chores before I could even get breakfast on the table. She had changed into her one good dress, and she was already helping to get the others ready too. To say she was anxious would not have done her feelings justice. Matthew and I sat at the table with the list of things we needed as he counted out silver coins from the money box.

"Could we spare money for some additional cloth? I need to add on to Mariah's dress again and Cordelia will need another dress soon too," I said as I looked at the small stack of coins.

"I think we can, we have eggs to sell. I will do two shoeings while we are there, so money for the girls and fifty cents for Kenneth for a new pair of pants. What would you like for yourself?"

"I want for nothing," I said smiling.

"Well, I know that is not true, but I thank you for saying it my dear," Matthew said as he kissed me and added another fifty cents to my pile with a wink.

We did not have much, it was true, but I felt like we had what we needed. Our parents had been very generous with furniture, bedding, and dishes when we left New York and I know Matthew's father Johan Wagner had given him some money with which to buy the land and start the farm. We were much better off than many. The Brownson family had lost their farm just last year after a fire took their barn and fields. Now, they live and work on the farm of the Morgans just down the road from us.

Finally ready, we all climbed into the wagon, and I held Charles on my lap as I rode alongside Matthew with Star and Moon hitched up to the lead. The children had named the horses and it made me smile every time we hitched them up together. Star was the bigger of the two, a large stud, black with white hooves and a star-like marking on his forehead. Moon, a little smaller, is our broodmare. She is my favorite and the one I seek out when I need solace and comfort when I do not want to burden Matthew. Her chestnut coat is smooth and soft, and I love to rub my cheek on her muzzle. We sold their colt last year and the money helped to make the winter months much easier. Hopefully, they will have another this year.

The road to town is rutted and muddy from the spring rains, but passable, and we jostle along for nearly two hours before buildings begin to appear on the horizon. Port Huron is a beautiful town which sits on the St. Clair River at the base of Lake Huron and the main part of town lies on land well elevated above the river. The town is divided by the Black River with nearly equal parts on each side. There are many large, beautiful trees and you can sit by the river for hours watching the steamers going up and down the river to places unknown. The main street is broad with shops on either side and a wide sidewalk to keep your feet dry and out of the mud.

Matthew drops us in front of the town square before he heads down to one of the stables to do his work for the day. As I had hoped, he has taken Kenneth with him to watch him work. Mariah holds on to Charles as he toddles along beside her and Rebecca holds on to Cordelia as we make our way to Cooks General Store and Trading Post. First, I will sell the eggs, and then we can shop for the things we need. I allow Cordelia to pick out the fabric she would like for her new dress, and she chooses a lovely blue check which will be a nice change from the solid brown she has now. Pants for Kenneth, a pair of socks for Matthew, a scrap of fabric to lengthen Mariah's dress, sugar, four hard candies (one for each child), and a few other food stores, and the budget was spent.

We wandered down to the little park near the river and set down to eat the small meal I had packed of chicken and bread with butter and watched the ships. Cordelia, Rebecca, and Charles ran back and forth across the grass laughing and rolling.

"Mother may I walk through town a bit?" asked Mariah.

"I don't see why not, but do not go off the main streets

please, and return at once if you see your father coming with the wagon," I said, and she kissed me on the cheek before running off.

I do not know how long we will keep her on the farm. She desires to be where things are more exciting and there are more people. I noticed when we were in Cooks that she kept glancing up at a boy who was there with his mother. I wonder if she has gone to see if he is still there. She's far too young for a beau but the headstrong nature of youth does not always follow the rules. When she leaves it will be difficult to manage, as Rebecca cannot be trusted to watch the littles and needs as much watching herself as Charles does. The poor girl. It is not her fault that she is rather dim-witted. It is as God intended it to be I suppose, but I do not know what kind of life she will have. I doubt very much she could be a wife and mother and so she will have to rely on her siblings when we are gone.

There is a man in the park standing on a box talking to a small crowd that has gathered about slavery in the South, its evil roots, and how it must be eradicated from our country. More and more the citizens of this nation seem divided by this issue. The plantation owners in the South rely on slave labor whereas in the North, it has been outlawed for over twenty years. People have help of course, but they are not slaves. They are paid, housed, or both. While I hear his voice carry over the breeze I pay it little attention. It is not an issue that concerns me.

It is lovely to have a few hours just to enjoy the sun and watch the river, but the sun is getting low in the sky. I gather up the children and walk back toward town. Mariah has not returned yet, but I am sure she is nearby and being watchful. She is very responsible and dutiful, and I have no doubt she will be ready to go when Matthew appears. We sit on the bench outside the bank, and I see Mariah is just down the street talking to a woman in a very fancy dress, something you would not normally see on the street this hour of the day. I do not know who she is. Perhaps just a chance encounter. When Mariah sees us, she comes right over.

"Who were you talking to Mariah?"

"Oh, that! Her name is Madame Parker. She was looking for her lost dog and she stopped me to see if I had seen him. She runs an inn at the edge of town."

"An inn?" I asked somewhat skeptically.

"So she says," shrugged Mariah as she quickly turned away.

I wonder if that is in fact the nature of her business, but perhaps Mariah is too naïve to suspect that this "inn" of hers might be something else entirely as her dress and salutation might suggest. I'm sure it was an innocent encounter but still, it left me with more suspicion than was probably Christian of me. I might mention it to Matthew to see if he knows who this woman is. As if on cue, Matthew turns the corner and stops in front of the bank. Once again, we pile into the wagon. Charles, being tired from the day's adventures, rides in the back with the rest of the children. Most of them are asleep before we reach the edge of town.

We rattle on toward the farm in companionable silence and we reach home just after the sun drops below the horizon but before the night closes in. Matthew finishes up the evening chores while I get a stew that has been simmering all day on the table. For a change, the children are in bed and asleep in their room early, and it gives me a chance to speak to Matthew about the woman, Madame Parker. As I explained to him what I had seen, I could tell he was bothered by Mariah's conversation.

"She is a woman of ill repute, and not someone that decent women, or men for that matter, should be talking to," he said nearly spitting out his words.

"So, her inn?"

Matthew scoffed. "It is a brothel Millicent, pure and simple. You need to tell Mariah that if that woman ever speaks to her again, she simply needs to turn and walk away, and cross the street if possible. She is to stay far away from Mrs. Parker lest others think that Mariah is associated with her."

"I will stress the importance of staying away from her," I said.

"See that you do," he replied somewhat angrily, before turning his attention to fixing a broken leg on the chair. He clearly did not want to speak of it any further and I let it go.

The spring gives way to summer and summer to fall. The post brings with it news from my sister Bessie that my mother has died in New York. This brings me great sadness and I find myself grieving intently. My mother was a strong, determined, and capable woman and I both admired her and did my best to emulate her. Her childhood was not an easy one. Fleeing the violence in France and having to start over in a new country is difficult even in the best of circumstances. She worked hard to learn the language and to help support her family. Some of my earliest memories are of her teaching me to cook and sew and she was an advocate for formal education for girls, unlike many of her contemporaries. Bessie and I both went to school until we were twelve even though many girls did not. My father will be lost without her, but I am glad James and Bessie are there for him.

She had the best laugh. Just hearing her laugh would bring

out smiles and laughter in others. She would laugh with her whole body, her eyes crinkling and shining, her shoulders heaving with the force of her merriment. She enjoyed her life and relished those moments of levity and just thinking of it brought a smile to my lips. I am despondent knowing I will never hear her laugh again, that my youngest children will not have strong memories of her. But I will do my best to keep her memory alive and we will speak her name often. In our family, we believe that by speaking someone's name and speaking well of them, you keep their spirit alive. I don't know where this tradition comes from, but my mother said it has been passed down through generations of women. Now it is my turn to see that this is done for her.

Bessie has also sent me a necklace that belonged to her, a small locket made of mother-of-pearl that had belonged to my grandmother and passed down from mother to daughter. I put it on immediately, feeling each one of the links with my fingers, the smoothness of the locket's face. It held a lock of my mother's hair. I held it tightly in my hand, grateful my sister had thought to do this for me. I will hold this close to my heart forever, a small bit of my mother always nearby.

Grieving will have to wait now as winter is nearly upon us. There is much to do to stock the larder and can and preserve the last of the garden. Mariah is an enormous help and

Rebecca even manages to entertain the little ones with a puppet made from an old sock. The leaves swirl outside the windows in circles as they fly from the safety of their branches to be swept up into the sky. The air has taken on that crispness which means the snow won't be far away. Soon our days will be filled with mending and sewing rather than planting and gardening, but I don't mind. I look forward to the respite that winter brings, although the house is beginning to feel smaller as the children grow. No matter. We will make do as there is not enough money to add on again, and as always, spring will be here again before we know it.

Chapter Two - *A New President*

The winter passes without much excitement and before we know it the air has taken on the warmth of a new season. But it is not just spring in Michigan. It is also the political season again, with an election for President of the United States coming up later this year. Matthew has always taken a keen interest in what is happening in the government. His father served in the New York legislature, and he often reads to me in the evening from the newspaper which gets passed around from neighbor to neighbor. Sometimes the news is a few weeks old, sometimes just a few days. It depends on how long it has been since someone went to town. I wonder had we stayed in New York if Matthew would have been interested in running for office himself. He speaks so well and is so smart. I am sure he would have done well had he chosen to do so.

Lizzie Brownson and Grace Morgan come often from the farm down the road, and the three of us share the news from town while we sew or churn. Lizzie is my beloved friend and it pained me so when she and her husband Thomas lost their farm, but I am glad she was able to stay on and work for Grace and David Morgan. It would have been a terrible loss for me if she had left Wales.

Newspapers are all talking of Abraham Lincoln as a potential Republican nominee for President and he is someone whom Matthew has admired since he ran for Congress a couple of years ago. He shares Matthew's strong conviction that slavery is an abomination. He even carefully cut from the newspaper one of Lincoln's speeches and he keeps it on the wall in a small frame.

A house divided against itself, cannot stand. I believe this government cannot endure permanently half slave and half free. I do not expect the Union to be dissolved – I do not expect the house to fall – but I do expect it will cease to be divided.

It will become all one thing or all the other. Either the opponents of slavery will arrest the further spread of it and place it where the public mind shall rest in the belief that it is in the course of ultimate extinction; or its advocates will push it forward, till it shall become lawful in all the States, old as well as new – North as well as South.

While I admired Matthew's stance on these issues of the day, I really take no interest in politics and honestly, I often tire easily when it is the topic of conversation. My mind instead is focused on my family, especially Mariah, as I can see more and more restlessness in her with every passing day. Grace's son Jeremiah who is eighteen seems to have an interest in her. I wonder if we let him court her if that would be enough to keep her feet firmly planted on this ground. I'll have to see what Matthew thinks. She is young to be married but a courtship could last for some time, and if the attention would keep her here longer it might be worth considering.

Mariah walks Cordelia and Kenneth to school while I clean up from breakfast. It has been a blessing to have a small school here in Wales so that I don't have to teach the children at home. Another year or so and Charles will be there too, leaving only Mariah and Rebecca home during the day. As I measure my life against how quickly the children are growing it seems as though each day is only a few hours. How can it be that my children are so old already? When did I become so old? It is as though time is in a hurry to get to a desti-nation I don't yet understand, a place in the future where life will be easier, I hope.

Today is mending day and I travel from basket to basket, going through the children's clothes to see what might need repair. I fixed a hole in one of Matthew's shirts last night and a buckle on his suspenders. He really needs a new pair of pants, but he defers to the needs of the children over his own; he always has. He will go into Port Huron tomorrow to get seed. Maybe I will see if I can talk him into doing something for himself while he is there.

Mariah helps with the mending. Her stitches are still a bit

unsure but functional. In time they will become more elegant but for now, I'm just grateful for the help.

"Mama, what is a brothel?" asked Mariah as she glanced up from her sewing.

Her question caught me so off guard that I nearly fell from my chair, and I brushed back my hair from my eyes buying myself a few precious seconds to formulate a reply.

"Why would you ask that?"

"I heard Papa say that Madam Parker's place was a brothel, but I don't understand what that means," she said with such innocence I was at a loss for what to say next. We had talked a little about womanhood when she began her flow last year, but not the relations between women and men.

I looked at her inquisitive face, "A brothel is a place where men go to have relations with women who are not their wives."

"But I thought Preacher Abrams said that relations are between a husband and wife, whatever relations are," she said thoughtfully.

"Yes, that is what the Bible says, but not everyone follows the Bible all of the time," I replied.

"And relations?"

It was clear I was not going to escape this conversation, and so we both put down our sewing and talked. She did not seem shocked. After all, we live on a farm and she has observed animals mating before, so she understood some already. Explaining the brothel and Madame Parker's role in it was a bit more delicate, but she seemed to comprehend my cursory explanation.

"So do you understand now why your father insisted that you should not speak with Madame Parker again?" I asked finally.

"Yes, I think so. Papa would not want anyone to think that I am a girl that does those things, the things they do there," she said.

"Yes, my darling, that is right, if you were to be thought of in that way it would dishonor you and our family, and your honor is something to be protected."

"It's time to collect the littles from school," I said, as I breathed a sigh of relief when she left the room. I hope I have done my duty as a mother and that I have imparted to her both the practical matters and the morality that comes with such things. I can't even begin to imagine trying to have this conversation with Rebecca. Perhaps, I won't have to. I doubt she will ever ask.

The next morning Matthew departed before the sun was up and that left me to milk while Mariah fed the littles and got them ready for school. Rebecca was mucking stalls and humming to herself as she always did. While she might not be the brightest child, she worked hard, generally without complaint. By the time I got back to the house, Mariah had returned from school and was clearing off the last of the breakfast dishes to the sink. We finished up together and then headed to the garden to prepare for the planting which would come in another few weeks. Weather this time of year can be unpredictable, and just when you think spring has arrived the snow makes a final appearance before loosening its grasp, making way for spring days.

Rebecca joined us and the three of us worked all morning, laughing and even singing a bit as we did so. It was more enjoyable than it should have been for as much work as had to be done.

"Mama," said Rebecca tugging on my sleeve.

I looked up from my task, "What?" I replied.

"There is man in the field," she said pointing north behind the house.

Sure enough, a man was walking slowly across the field toward the house, and he was a man I did not recognize.

"Into the house girls quickly. Go to my room and lock the door," I said as we nearly ran across the yard to the house. I grabbed the rifle from off the wall by the door and checked to make sure it was loaded before stepping out on the back porch. The man seemed to have a pack on his back, and he was walking slowly as he looked around. I don't think he could see me just yet, the sun being in his eyes, but I watched him carefully. Perhaps he was just walking through the woods looking for a road? I stayed quiet holding tightly onto the gun which felt heavy in my hands. As I watched, he turned and began to move in my direction. I stepped away from the house so he could see me more clearly and see that I was armed. Maybe that would dissuade him from coming too close. My heart was beating fast, and my hands were getting clammy, so I wiped them on my apron. I could ill afford to lose my grip on this gun.

He raised his arm in salutation and continued moving closer. I waited till he exited the field and started across the yard.

"I think that is far enough, stranger," I said as I raised the rifle.

"No need to fear ma'am, I am just passing through," he said as he removed his hat.

He looked to be in his late teens or maybe early twenties. And while his clothes were store-bought, he was rather dirty and scruffy, but his bright blue eyes were clear and twinkled as he smiled.

"You are trespassing on our land," I said firmly.

"My apologies, ma'am. I am trying to find my way to Port Huron," he said as he shuffled his feet.

"Walk past the house and you will find a dirt road. If you take that north east it will take you to Port Huron," I replied.

"Thank you, ma'am. I'm in need of food. Is there any work I could do for you in exchange for a meal?" he said hopefully.

I lowered the rifle. I did not see a weapon although he did have a bag that could have held a pistol. He did not seem to be a threat and the Christian thing to do would be to at least feed him before I sent him on his way.

"If you chop some firewood, I will provide you with some food to take with you on your journey," I said as I pointed to the woodpile.

"I am most grateful ma'am," he said as he quickly dropped his pack and went to work immediately on the pile.

I stepped into the house locking the door behind me.

"Mariah, it is safe come out," I called out as I watched the man through the window. The girls peeked out over my shoulder to get a better look.

"Who is he?" asked Rebecca.

"No one, he is just passing through on his way to Port Huron. He is chopping wood in exchange for some food."

The girls peered out the window at him. We didn't get

many strangers in this area.

"Mariah, keep an eye on him while I pack up some food. Let me know if he approaches the house," I said as I set to work on my task.

I need not have asked. While Rebecca wandered away to something else, Mariah could not take her eyes off the young man, watching his every move as though she had never seen a man chop wood before. I chuckled to myself. It is the age of infatuation and I remember it well, the heart-fluttering, stammering phase, when all girls feel like they could be prettier.

"Mariah, take this to the young man please, and tell him he can wash up and fill his canteen at the well," I said, as I handed her the meal I had wrapped in a small cloth.

Delighted, she scampered off as I once again picked up the rifle and stood on the back porch. I don't think he represents a threat, but you can never be sure of a man's character. I watched carefully as he and Mariah exchanged a few words. He seemed very polite, and she grinned from ear to ear, as did he. I'm sure they would have chatted longer, but chores needed to be done and I could not do them while standing watch.

"Mariah, come on to the house now," I said loudly.

"Thank you, ma'am, for your hospitality. It is much

appreciated, and may God bless you and your family," said the man loudly and with a slight bow.

I nodded my acceptance of his blessing as Mariah joined me on the porch. We watched as he passed by, and Mariah ran to the front of the house to watch him through the front window as he started down the road. At one point she waved, presumably in reply, and I smiled. Oh, to be young again. I love Matthew with all my heart and our union is a good one, but there is nothing like the murmurings of the young heart.

When Matthew returned that evening Mariah could not help but regale him with all the details of our day, especially those of the young man whose name, it turns out, is John. I had not seen her so animated before and laughter punctuated her tale every few minutes. While he was grateful for having one less chore to do, I could see the concern in his eyes that we had been here alone when a stranger approached.

Matthew was also excited as all the news from town centered on the race for President and there are now four men whose names will be on the ballot. Stephen Douglass, a Senator from Illinois representing the Northern Democratic Party, and John Breckenridge representing the Southern Democratic Party. Since the Democratic party is fractured between North and South, they have put two candidates forward. The Tennessee politician John Bell representing the

Constitutional Party and Abraham Lincoln, as had been anticipated, for the Republican Party.

Matthew had already decided he was going to support Mr. Lincoln if he was put forward, and he was quite pleased at this development. The election, however, was stirring once again the specter of secession as many of the slave states have said they would secede if a Republican was elected president.

"Matthew, you don't really believe that the Southern states that allow slavery will leave and break off, do you?" I asked, clearly skeptical. He looked past me, as if trying to see the future in the distance, a vision not in clear focus.

"I'm afraid I do. This moral and practical debate on slavery is not going away and the Southern states have made it clear they will not give on this issue. There is a real fear in the South that a Northern president might come and take their slaves, leaving them no way to work their land and support their way of life."

"Surely not more than a couple of states would make that choice."

"South Carolina is the most vocal of all the Southern states and I suspect they will lead the way. Beyond that Mississippi, Alabama, Florida, Georgia… it's hard to say," he said as he rubbed his eyes and shook his head as if to deny his very words.

"What will happen if they do?"

"Ah my dear, that remains to be seen but I doubt if elected President Lincoln would allow it to stand. It's hard to say about some of the others, but he has been clear that we are one United States of America and secession would be seen as an act of war."

"Goodness, Matthew, a war between the states would be catastrophic," I replied, my eyes wide as the horror of it started to sink in.

"It could be, but let's not think on it now. Perhaps it will not happen, and we need to focus on the farm and our own for now," he said as he rose from his chair and put his arms around me, holding me close. I lay my head on his chest and despite his warmth, I shuddered, closing my eyes as if doing so would keep out the future I did not want to even imagine, but it still hung in my mind terrifyingly clear.

Spring on the farm is always a joyous time, although also a time when the work is endless and grueling. We've decided to plant a bit less acreage this year to help make the burden more manageable. Matthew's blacksmithing has been most profitable, and we can step back from the farm just a bit. As I had hoped, Jeremiah has been spending some time at our house and Mariah seems to enjoy his presence. Truly his mother and I conspired, but the children need not know. Charles is doing his best to run after the older children, but his efforts generally end with him being face down in the dirt, about which he does not fuss. He gets up and tries again, especially if his goal is the pen that holds the newborn lamb, his favorite these days.

Rebecca is maturing in body, if not mind, and I worry that she may fall prey to young men who wish to take advantage of her naivety and lack of understanding. She is worse at some times than others it seems, although I know not the reason why. It requires watching her even more intently but how we will continue to accomplish that, I do not know.

"My love, I'm going into town tomorrow with the Morgans. I need just a few things and Grace has invited me to join them," I said to Matthew as we climbed into bed.

"Of course. Mariah can manage I think with Cordelia and Kenneth at school. I'll do my best to keep an eye on Rebecca too," he said as he kissed me goodnight and turned over with a weary sigh.

The work of the farm is so hard, and I wish we could afford more help. Perhaps next year. I turn on my side to face him and move close to the warmth his body offers as I rest my cheek along his back. I'm nearly asleep when I feel a tug on the blanket.

"Mama, I'm thirsty," said Charles rubbing his eyes with his little fists.

"Come here my dear," I said as I gathered him into our bed and gave him a drink from the cup I kept on the table.

He drank noisily, slurping the water, then wiping his face on the sheet.

"Stay Mama?" he said hopefully.

"Yes, you may, now sleep and don't wake your father," I whispered as I tucked him in between Matthew and me. He was asleep in an instant and as I stroked his hair, I thought about having another baby. I know Matthew feels we cannot manage anymore, especially with Rebecca, but life does not always do as we would wish. We shall see.

Grace Morgan knocked quietly on the door as the sun was just starting to filter through the trees. We needed to get an early start so that her husband David could be back in time to finish the chores before sunset. Jeremiah and Thomas would look after things until then. I slipped out the door, careful not to wake the children. Matthew was already out in the barn, and he whistled and waved as I climbed up into the wagon next to Grace. I waved back as David turned the horses up the road. We had thought we could get what we needed in Wales, but there had been a small fire at the general store there and things were not yet back to normal. The journey to Port Huron is much longer, but I don't mind it, and the forest on either side of the road greets us with the bright green of spring. Small wildflowers fight for the shafts of sunlight filtering through the trees and the sounds of birds fill the air.

The three of us chatted about the news of the day as we rattled along… the election, the birth of a new baby at the Johnson farm, and the new deacon at church. Our conversation makes the trip go quickly and we are tying up in town just as the sun makes itself known at the tops of the trees. David and Grace head toward the law office as I wait for Cook's Store to open, chatting with a few of the other women who are also waiting. A young man on a chestnut mare ties up outside the store as well and while he seems vaguely familiar, I cannot quite place him. He is clean-shaven and well-dressed in fine clothes, but it is the blue of his eyes that finally sparks recognition. It is the young man who walked through our property just a few days ago. My, how his fortunes have changed in such a short time.

"Ma'am," he said, tipping his hat as he stopped to open the door which had just been unlocked at the general store.

"John, is it?" I asked.

"Yes ma'am, John Parker. It is a pleasure to see you as I

get to thank you again for your hospitality when I crossed your land," he said with a lopsided grin.

"You are welcome. Parker, you said is your family name?"

"Yes ma'am, my Aunt Martha Parker owns the inn just outside of town. I've come here to work for her. I apologize I did not learn your name when we last met," he said looking at me expectantly.

I could feel myself blushing remembering what Matthew had said about the Parker inn. I realized now that I did not want to be seen with this man, nor did I want to be rude.

"Mrs. Wagner," I said as I nodded my thanks, slipping through the open door hoping he would not follow me inside.

"Good day to you then, Mrs. Wagner," he said tipping his hat as the door closed behind me.

A huge sigh of relief escaped me as I watched him continue down the sidewalk. I could only hope that Grace and David had not seen me talking to him, or if they did, that they did not know who he was. In just under an hour, we were back on the road toward home. I did not mention the encounter and it was not brought up, so I could assume that it was not seen. I can't imagine what Matthew will think when I tell him what I've learned about John. I'm sure he will not be pleased. Perhaps I need not. I doubt very much that this young man will matter in our lives ever again.

The days pass in our quiet routine, and other than the new home being built across the way from our farm, the world is unchanged. The hammering is a constant companion from dawn to dusk and the house, a rather large one, is taking shape quickly. Matthew has spoken to the men who have been there working, they are building the house for a family moving up from Detroit who wish to live a quieter life than the city can offer. They will certainly have that here, for very little happens in our little enclave and quiet is the order of the day.

The summer is warm and dry but not so dry as to damage the crops and harvesting will be starting soon. It seems as I age the seasons get shorter and shorter. Wasn't it just a few weeks ago the flowers made their first appearance? While the weather may be starting to cool, the race for President seems to heat up more and more every day. It is all anyone can talk about and as the election draws near there is much debate about the consequences of our choice. John Breckinridge running as a Southern Democrat seemed to have widespread support across the South, but in the four-way race, it was impossible to predict what would happen.

Abraham Lincoln has been paired with Hannibal Hamlin, a respected politician from Maine who supports Lincoln's ideas regarding slavery. Hamlin was once a Democrat, and it was hoped he would bring with him voters from that party for the cause. Matthew had even gone to hear him speak when he came to Detroit, and he was pleased with what he heard.

"Lincoln and Hamlin are going to change this country for the better, I am most sure of it," he said as he stacked some firewood next to the stove.

"But what of the South, Matthew? Surely, we must elect someone who can lead the whole country, not just the North," I said warily.

"It is true that there is no affection between the South and his ideas about slavery, but he will persuade them, I am sure."

But others were far less sure and there was still much talk of unrest in the South. Still, our days were filled with work on the harvest. Issues of the day faded into the background as we worked tirelessly. There was a good crop this year and we will have much to take to market. The wagon will be groaning under the weight of all the bushels of corn. The election is on November 6th so we will wait a week later than usual to go into Port Huron. Matthew can sell first, then go to vote while I gather up the things we will need for the winter, this being our last trip into town until spring. Hopefully, the rain will stay away or turn to snow so that the roads do not become impassable.

"Mother why can't I go into town with you?" whined Mariah, crossing her arms angrily as she plopped into the chair next to me.

"Mariah, I've told you, several times now, there is no room for more than your father and I, and so you'll need to stay with the children."

"We can fit three in front if we try! Why can't Mrs. Brownson watch them?"

I wiped my face on my apron, the beads of sweat trickling down the sides of my temples from the heat of the stove. I loved this girl, but she could surely be trying.

"Mariah, it is our responsibility to care for ourselves. We should only depend on others when it is very necessary so as not to risk alienating our friends and neighbors. Otherwise, when we truly need them, they may not be there for us."

"I hate this place!" she said as she angrily stormed out the back door. I watched as she stomped all the way to the barn.

"Why doesn't Mariah like us?" said Rebecca as she and Cordelia came into the kitchen. Clearly, they had heard us from the bedroom.

"Oh, my darling girl, it's not that she doesn't like you. She just wants to have a more exciting life than we can manage."

"I don't like her anymore," replied Rebecca with a very serious tone.

"Now, Rebecca. That is very unchristian of you. Mariah is your sister, so of course you like her. I agree that you may not always like what she does, or says, but that doesn't mean that you don't like her."

"Yes, it does," she replied with that childlike innocence of hers.

"I don't like her either," said Cordelia.

"Enough now girls. I'll hear no more talk like this. Now, Rebecca go and fetch Mariah from the barn and you girls wash up for supper. Tell the boys to wash and help Charles."

They ran off hand in hand toward the barn as I turned my attention to getting food on the table. I don't know what we are going to do to keep Mariah happy here, but we need to find a way to be sure.

The morning of November 6th was cold but dry and we set off as soon as Mariah was up and getting breakfast ready. The Morgans were also heading into town as were several of the other families and we gathered in a caravan of seven wagons in all. The town was bustling with more people than I had ever seen, and wagons were lined up for nearly half a mile outside of the market warehouse. This was going to be a long day to be sure. Lizzie, Grace, Mrs. James (who I do not know well), and Mrs. Whitsitt who had just moved into the new house across the street joined me in Cook's General Store which was bursting at the seams with women shopping while their husbands vote or sell. It was almost a festive atmosphere with much talk and laughter. Mrs. Cook was even giving samples of a new licorice that I found quite enjoyable. I might be able to find a few cents to take some back to the children.

It took quite some time to get through the line but finally, we all managed to get the things we needed loaded into our flour sacks. The Morgans had brought two wagons, and one was offloaded quickly so that it could come to the store to collect all our purchases until we were ready to head home. We had not anticipated the day would be so long. None of us had packed enough food, and what we had we left with the men. Grace bought a couple of biscuits we were going to share.

"Ladies, why don't we have lunch at the Petit Café?" said Mrs. Whitsitt.

The Petit family was one of the earliest families to settle in this area before Port Huron was even formed, and they had opened a small café near the train station. I looked nervously at Lizzie. I knew she could not afford it; I wasn't sure that I could either, but I did not want her to be embarrassed.

"Mrs. Whitsitt I'm afraid I will have to decline. I have other plans, but you ladies go on and enjoy yourselves," I said smiling as I took Lizzie's hand and squeezed it.

"I'm going with Millicent," said Lizzie as she smiled at me, grateful for the excuse I had created.

"Surely your other errands can wait. Please come, as my guests of course," said Mrs. Whitsitt.

I looked at Grace. "Yes, please do come," she said.

"Mrs. Whitsitt that is most generous of you. Truly you need not do that, but Lizzie and I are most grateful for your offer."

"I insist," said Mrs. Whitsitt as she put her arm through mine. "I wish to get to know you ladies better and this is a perfect opportunity," she said as she steered me toward the station.

I looked over my shoulder to see Grace, Lizzie, and Mrs. James all falling in step behind us. Mrs. Whitsitt is clearly someone used to getting her way.

"Mrs. Whitsitt, I cannot thank you enough for your generous invitation," I said as we walked along the wooden sidewalk arm in arm.

"My pleasure, Mrs. Wagner… and please call me

Charlotte," she said as she squeezed my arm.

"Millicent, but most of my friends call me Millie."

"A beautiful name," she replied.

Mrs. Whitsitt, Charlotte, was impeccably dressed and I felt quite dowdy and plain next to her. Her bodice was heavily embroidered with small flowers set against a crimson silk fabric and around her shoulders a beautiful woolen shawl that complemented her dress. Her hair was tucked up into a lovely hat with a large collection of silk flowers and netting. Even Grace's clothing paled by comparison. Up until the Whitsett family moved in, the Morgans had been the most well-to-do family in our area. Mrs. James, Lizzie, and I were in our best, but still, we did not hold a candle to Charlotte.

The café was lovely, and every table was filled but after Charlotte spoke to someone, a table was set for us near the back of the room. There were a few people with small pieces of luggage who were waiting for the train, but most seemed to be people from town, many more women than men. I had never eaten in a café before, and it was a treat to have someone cook and serve me for a change, but a pleasure I must not get used to. It would cost nearly two dollars for all of us to eat but Charlotte seemed to have no concern about the expense.

The food was wonderful, a stew of some sort, with crusty

bread and a delicious cake for dessert, and tea. The conversation flowed easily, and it was fascinating to learn more of Charlotte's life which had certainly been more interesting than any of ours. Her husband, Leo, had an important position with the railroad and they had traveled extensively through the United States. They had even honeymooned in London, which was beyond my imagination. They had been married for twenty years but had no living children. We could all see this was a source of pain for her, so we did not probe. We all understood too well the agony of losing a child.

The afternoon passed quickly, and I forgot that Lizzie and I had declined the luncheon invitation under the guise of other errands. I'm sure she must have known the real reason for my reluctance, but to her credit, she did not mention it, and neither did Lizzie or me. After lunch, we wandered up and down the street looking in the windows of all the shops, but it was quickly getting colder as the sun dropped below the trees. Thankfully, just as we were considering where to take some shelter, the wagons could be seen coming down the street stopping in front of Cooks, which is our designated meeting place.

"Thank you again, Charlotte, for the luncheon. It was so very thoughtful of you," I said as we prepared to board the wagons.

"Of course, please call on me during the winter. Company always makes the dreary days go by more quickly," she said smiling.

"I will, I promise," I replied as Matthew helped me into the wagon.

I was grateful for the blankets we kept in the wagon, and Matthew lit the lantern which also put out a bit of heat. It was fully dark now and we moved slowly along the road. Suddenly, Star and Moon whinnied loudly as they came to a halt.

From the darkness of the trees, a herd of deer darted out and ran across the road right in front of us. There must have been twenty or thirty of them racing across the road back into the safety of the forest. The horses weren't the only ones startled and I nearly dropped the lantern before breaking out into a nervous laughter that soon had Matthew laughing too. I wasn't sure if he was laughing at me or with me, but either way, it kept us giggling all the way home. Matthew dropped me at the house before heading to the barn where Star and Moon would get their long-awaited feed. As I came into the kitchen my heart sank. There were dirty dishes and food all over the table. The fire in the hearth was barely going.

I walked into the bedroom and found all the children

asleep, some still in their clothes, with dirty faces and hands. It was too much, and I sat down on the end of Kenneth's bed and cried quietly. I thought about waking Mariah but decided I could not face her anger tonight. I made sure everyone was covered and then closed the door behind me as the chaos of the kitchen lay before me. I made quick work of it, and nearly all was well by the time Matthew came from the barn. He was tired and so was I. This was a conversation for another day. As I finally lay down to sleep my thoughts turned to just one thing… Mariah.

Chapter Three - *United No More*

It has been nearly a month since the election and word has finally reached us. Lincoln and Hamlin have won. Matthew is elated as are most in the North, but the newspaper warns of consequences which they believe will come soon. Mariah has been sullen and difficult for weeks after having been punished with extra chores after her gross neglect when caring for the children. Still, we did our best to celebrate her sixteenth birthday and I surprised her with a whole bolt of cloth for a new dress which I bought during my last trip to town. Matthew has made her a beautiful trinket box with her initials carved into the lid and these gifts do seem to lighten her mood finally, especially since I invited Jeremiah Morgan to join us for the celebration. His gift of a dried flower bouquet tied up with lovely ribbons was very pretty, and Mariah blushed when he gave it to her.

It is a shame that Mariah's birthday is so close to the visit of Father Christmas as it usually means she receives less for the holiday, having just been given gifts earlier in the month. All the other children are born in the spring or early fall, so she is the only one who is at such a disadvantage, but there is nothing I can do. The money box is fuller than it has been in a long time, but we must conserve it because we never know how the harvest will be from year to year. Perhaps Matthew can consider something else for her when he is shoeing next week.

The girls and I focus on baking for the holiday, and Cordelia is excited to be a bigger part of the process this year. At the age of ten, she is tall and able to stand at the stove without the smaller stool. We laugh and talk while we work and it's the first time in some months I feel we are at peace with each other. The girl's laughter warms my heart. Even Rebecca is doing well following directions, and the biscuits and cakes are coming together nicely.

"Cordelia, you are stepping on my foot," Rebecca said

sternly.

"I'm sorry sissy. I did not mean to," said Cordelia meekly.

"You are such a bad child, bad, bad, bad," Rebecca said as she grabbed Cordelia's hand and pushed it against the hot stove.

The smell of burning flesh filled my nostrils.

"No!" I screamed at Rebecca as I pushed her away, grabbing Cordelia up in my arms. She was screaming and crying as I hurried to the sink and plunged her hand into some cold water.

"It's going to be alright baby, it's alright, I know it hurts," I said to Cordelia as she nestled her face into my neck with her tears running onto my chest.

"Mariah, fetch your father and hurry. Rebecca, go to the bedroom and stay there until I come to speak to you," I said angrily.

"What can I do?" said Matthew as he hurried into the kitchen.

"Here, take her. I need to get an egg," I said as I handed Cordelia to her father. "And you need to pat the burn dry. It's going to hurt."

I could see the anguish in Matthew's eyes knowing he had to inflict this pain on his youngest daughter. He held her tightly with one arm while he dabbed at the burn with the other. Mariah talked soothingly to her while I separated an egg into a bowl and whipped up the egg whites. They would form a barrier over the burn allowing it to heal, but it would be painful for some time.

"Matthew?"

"Yes, I know. Mariah, get the whisky from the cabinet in the front room. Hurry."

I put a bit of milk in with the whiskey and some sugar and whisked it together before I handed it to Matthew.

"You need to drink this little one. It might not taste good, but it will make your hand better, so you need to stop crying. Can you do that for me?"

Cordelia gulped the air as she tried to get her sobs to subside, her face red and her eyes swollen. Finally, she was able to drink, and she consumed the contents of the glass in just a couple of swallows.

"Mariah, get a couple of strips of cloth from the sewing basket. Find the material we use for petticoats," I said as I pulled a chair up next to Matthew who was still holding Cordelia.

"This is going to hurt you my darling and I am sorry, but we need to do this and then, it will start to feel better."

The whiskey was already starting to work on her. She was crying less and seemed calmer. Slowly I covered the burn with the egg whites. It was an angry, deep red line extending nearly all the way across the upper part of her palm. I wrapped it up carefully after the egg whites had dried. She was so brave and cried only a little before laying her head on her father's chest closing her eyes, exhausted and feeling the whiskey more and more.

"Put her in our room," I said as Matthew rose carefully from the chair trying not to disturb her.

"Mama," said Charles as he climbed onto my lap. He was frightened by all the crying and screaming, his own tears coming through but I'm sure he did not really know why.

"You are alright my child, and so is Cordelia. Everything will be well, you will see," I said as I held him close to me.

"Let me take him, Mother," said Mariah, reaching for him.

I was grateful for her help and handed him off to her. Kenneth stood quietly against the wall having said nothing this whole time.

"Why don't you get Kenneth and Charles something to eat while I check on Cordelia," I said to Mariah as I ruffled Kenneth's hair on the way to my room. He was such a quiet boy. While he could certainly speak well, he seemed to have little to say, which was so different from the girls.

Matthew was sitting on the edge of the bed his hand

resting on Cordelia's back. She seemed to be asleep as her breathing was coming slow and regular.

"What happened?" asked Matthew as I sat down beside him on the bed.

I told him the details, not that there was much to tell. It seemed that whenever Rebecca acted out it was toward Cordelia, but this was the first time she had done something beyond the simple taunts and hitting that often occurs between siblings.

"Is this going to heal?" asked Matthew as he stroked Cordelia's hair.

"Yes, the burn will heal, although it will not be quick. Her heart may take even more time. She will be very angry with her sister."

Matthew sighed as he turned to look at me, his brow knitted together in consternation as he took my hands in his.

"What are we going to do about Rebecca? There seems to be this malevolent spirit in her and I do not understand where it comes from."

"I do not know," I said quietly. "I just do not know."

Two days later, as things were just beginning to get back to some semblance of normal, there was a knock at the door. It was David Morgan.

"David, is everything alright?" I asked as I ushered him into the parlor.

"Is Matthew here?" he asked with a sense of urgency.

"Yes, he's in the barn. Let me send one of the children for him. Can I get you some water?"

"No thank you. I'm fine," he said, but he didn't seem fine as he nervously rung his hands as he waited by the door, refusing to sit down.

"David," said Matthew wiping his hands off on a towel before shaking hands with him. "What did you need?"

He looked at me, then back to Matthew. I could tell he was reluctant to speak in front of me so I excused myself to the kitchen, but I could still hear some of what was said.

"What!" exclaimed Matthew.

"It's true. I heard it at the courthouse today when I was there. It was the headline in a paper a man traveling from New York had with him. He showed it to several men," he said solemnly.

"Thank you for letting me know. I will be in town for shoeing after Christmas and I will see if there is more news," said Matthew as he shook hands again with David before closing the door behind him. When I walked into the parlor, he was leaning against the front door, his hands on his legs as he leaned forward slightly.

"Matthew, what is it?" I asked anxiously. He spoke without even looking up.

"South Carolina. They have determined that it is no longer in their best interest to remain in the Union, and they have declared their secession from the United States," he replied haltingly as he stood up.

"But Lincoln hasn't even been sworn in yet!"

"No, but he has always made his position clear, and they are claiming that there is an increasing hostility directed toward the slave-holding states by the states where slavery is outlawed. Their statement claims we have elected someone who is hostile to the South who will destroy their way of life."

I sat down in the chair, my legs feeling as if they could no longer hold my weight.

"What does this mean Matthew? What is going to happen?"

"I've no doubt this means war, a civil war between the North and the South," he said despondently.

"Surely not," I said shaking my head in disbelief.

"It's nearly Christmas. Let's not talk of it in front of the children. They need to enjoy this holiday season. Time will tell, and soon, if anything will come of it."

He was right. It did not take long. Ten days after South Carolina, Mississippi announced they too would secede. Then the very next day Florida, and the day after Alabama. A week later Georgia and then Louisiana. By the end of January six states had left the United States. In February it was Texas and in April, Virginia.

"Millicent, I need to go into Port Huron tomorrow," said Matthew as he sat down to supper.

"Why? We still have planting to do. What could be so urgent in town?"

I could see he was hesitant. Perhaps he did not want to speak in front of the children.

"We can speak after supper," I said quickly as he nodded, turning his attention to the chicken and potatoes on his plate.

"Mother, can I go with Father? I could do any shopping you may need," said Mariah hopefully.

After the unpleasant experience we had in November when we left Mariah with the children she has not been away from the house. Maybe it would be good to let her go with Matthew, and she is certainly capable of getting the few things I need.

"Your father and I will discuss it," I replied, and that seemed to satisfy her.

Cordelia is still very hesitant to be near Rebecca and she keeps her distance from her as best she can. Her hand has healed very well, just a small scar, but a constant reminder of what her sister did to her. Her heart, however, is still very much wounded, and even Rebecca recognizes that their relationship has been forever changed. I think it would not be good to leave them so perhaps sending Mariah to town with Matthew is the right choice.

"So, what did you not want to say in front of the children?" I asked when we were finally alone.

"President Lincoln has put out a call for seventy-five thousand militia to put down the rebellion. Men from all around St. Clair County are gathering in Port Huron to talk about forming up. Also, Arkansas and North Carolina have seceded as well."

I couldn't help but gasp out loud and I quickly covered my mouth with my hand to stifle any further outburst. Surely, he was not thinking of joining the militia. I could feel my heart racing as its pounding echoed in my ears.

"Sit down my dear, you look unsteady," he said as he guided me to the chair.

"Please tell me you are not going to join the militia?" I asked as the tears welled up in my eyes.

"Millie, you know this fight against slavery is one I feel passionately about, and we must support the President in this effort. We cannot allow states to come and go from the Union. It has not even been a hundred years since we broke away from England and to be fractured in this way is not good. Having a potential enemy on our doorstep would be ill-advised. Besides, we need their cotton and produce. They are things we can't grow in these northern climates."

"But surely the South would never turn on the Northern states to try and overtake us?" I replied, shaking my head in disbelief that we were even having this talk.

"They are prepared to fight to protect their way of life. Their monetary livelihood is clear, so what is to stop them from someday turning on us in full?"

I couldn't speak. The words felt like ash in my throat, and I was unable to get them out. We sat there looking at each other, knowing deep in our hearts what this might mean.

"I know what a hardship it would be on you, on any woman, whose husband leaves her to join the fighting. But by all accounts, the government seems to think this will be over in just a few weeks. I could be back in no time."

"Or you might not come back at all..." I replied my voice trailing off to a whisper as I stared at my lap.

"That is in God's hands," he said as he stroked my hair, then lifted my chin so that he could look at me. "I can promise you that I will not go if there are plenty of men who volunteer but if we as a community agree we must do more, then I will have no choice. Never could I look you, or my children, in the eye again if I did not do my duty to my country and this cause."

I wanted to cry. I wanted to beg him on my hands and knees not to go. Above all Matthew believes in doing what is right, what is just, and what he feels God expects of him. What I expect of him, what the children need from him, is important no doubt… but not as important as being true to himself and the man he is. I loved him for that, but at this moment, I wished it were not so.

They set off just as the sun was rising. David Morgan and Thomas Brownson went with them on horseback as well as several other men from Wales. I did my best to busy myself throughout the day with chores, trying not to think about what might be happening in town. I attacked mucking the stalls with a vigor that was fed by anger and frustration, stabbing my pitchfork into the hay with such force that had a mouse been hiding in the straw it would not have stood a chance. My arms were aching, but I did not stop stabbing repeatedly, as if in doing so I could kill the fear as if it were a creature. I felt it creeping up my back, the hair on my neck standing on end as it overtook me, engulfing me in its clutches.

Finally exhausted, I dropped to my knees and cried. My tears came in a torrent for all those men who might die trying to quell this rebellion, and for all the women who would be left alone when it was over. Would I be one of them?

The children had gone to bed by the time they returned home, and Mariah stopped only to eat a bit before she too was in bed. Matthew waited until the bedroom door was closed before he spoke. Surely it was only ten minutes, but it felt like ten hours. My palms were sweaty and my nerves raged.

"I did not enlist today," said Matthew finally.

I could feel myself relax, my shoulders dropping down into a more normal position, but it was clear at once that there was more to it.

"There were enough men who were willing to go today, including David Morgan. I told them if the conflict extends past the harvest that I will join the fight."

"David is going right away?"

"Yes, he has a couple of days to gather some things then he and another twenty or so men will be headed for Detroit to meet up with others. He will join the existing Army cavalry unit as will the other men who are on horseback. Those without horses will join the infantry."

"This will not take more than a few weeks, will it?" I asked holding my breath, fearful of his reply.

"Do not be so sure. Four days ago, South Carolina attacked Fort Sumter in Charleston Harbor and the Union forces there have already surrendered."

"How can that be!" I cried out horrified by that news.

"Astonishing, I know, but it speaks to the commitment of the Confederated States to defend slavery," he said wearily.

Never have I seen Matthew looking so despondent, not

even when we suffered a stillborn child. I am sure he wanted to go, and I am very grateful he did not. I can see that this decision was very difficult for him. Excruciating, even.

"There is something else, too," he said after a moment.

"About David?"

"No, about Mariah," he said as he rose and began pacing around the room.

"Did something happen when you were in town?" I said hesitantly.

"When I returned to fetch her from Cooks Store, she was waiting outside as I had instructed, but she was not waiting alone. There was a young man with her. She introduced him to me as one John Parker."

"Yes, he is the young man who came through the farm some time ago when you were in town. He met Mariah when she took some food out to him, but they only spoke for a few minutes, and I watched from the window to be sure nothing improper occurred," I said quickly.

"He is the nephew of Madame Parker I understand?"

"Yes. I also saw him the last time I was in town with the Morgans. I did not recognize him at first as he was wearing nice clothes and was clean-shaven, but he did speak to me to thank me again for my kindness when he was passing through."

"He has asked if he can write to Mariah," said Matthew bluntly.

I stared at my husband, knowing at once what his response would be given his profound disapproval of Madame Parker and her business.

"You told him no?"

"I did, and I must say Mariah was not pleased with me, but I will stand firm on this Millicent. I do not want anyone in this family, least of all my daughter, associated with those people."

"Of course, I agree with you completely. Besides, I am hoping that she will entertain a true courtship with Jeremiah

Morgan soon."

Matthew shook his head. "I think she enjoys his company, but it seems to me she treats him almost as an older brother which does not bode well for courting."

"Perhaps not, but I can see that Jeremiah certainly has an interest in her," I replied.

"Time will tell but either way. I am in no hurry for her to move on with him too quickly, as she is still young."

"I was only three years older than her age when I had her," I said lightheartedly.

Matthew smiled. "Yes, I know dearest, but our daughter is not you," he said as he undressed and climbed into bed.

Despite the quiet and the light rain on the roof, we slept little, as my husband tossed and turned all night long, finally rising before the sun was even up. There was no point in my staying in bed either, so I rose as well and began making breakfast. The children trickled in one after the other, Charles climbing up on his father's lap when he came in from the barn to tell him all about the tadpole he had found yesterday in the pond. There was laughter and the sound of children's voices talking over each other, vying for their parents' attention. My heart was warmed by the scene, but I could not help but wonder how many more of these moments we might have. I shook my head. No, I can't think this way. I must believe this conflict will be over quickly and that Matthew will never need to go.

David stopped on his way south and Matthew checked the shoes on his horse, changing out a few nails and making sure the horse's hooves were clean and in good repair. A lame horse was something he could ill afford. I could see the guilt in Matthew's eyes. However, David had something we did not… an older son in Jeremiah. He could keep things going on the farm with Thomas Brownson and his younger siblings. While Mariah can be of great help, it is different from having a young man do the physical work of farming. Still, this would be most difficult for Grace, and I must remember to call on her soon. I'm sure she is as fearful as I would be. Lizzie and I must do our best to support her.

News came in mid-May that United States forces had crossed the Potomac River, and they were occupying the area known as Arlington Heights as well as nearby Alexandria. A flag of the Confederated States had been flying for a few weeks from the roof of the Marshall House, which is an inn that is so large it could be seen by a spyglass from the White House. Colonel Elmer Ellsworth, who was leading a regiment of volunteers from New York into the area, wanted the flag removed at once. He climbed the stairs of the inn himself to take it down. Unfortunately, on his way back down the stairs, the proprietor, one James Jackson who is a fervent defender of slavery, ambushed him from one of the rooms. He killed Ellsworth with a round fired from a shotgun at close range. One of Ellsworth's men waiting below rushed up the stairs and killed Jackson.

A reporter from the *New York Tribune* was traveling along

with the troops so news of the shooting travelled fast. But Ellsworth was not just any officer. He was also a friend of Abraham Lincoln's, having worked as a law clerk in his Springfield office before following him to Washington. When the President learned of his death, he was terribly aggrieved, and he insisted that his body be brought to the Capital where he lay in state for several days before his body was taken to New York City. Thousands lined the streets to view the funeral cortège.

Elmer Ellsworth was just twenty-four years old, engaged to be married, and a most admired and respected young man whose life was taken much too soon. He might have been the first Union officer to be killed, but he certainly would not be the last.

Chapter Four - *The Heartbreak to Come*

Richmond, Virginia, has now become the capital of what most refer to as the Confederacy, although others use foul words that a fair woman would not repeat. David has been gone for over a month now and Grace has had no word from him.

"Do you have any idea where he might be?" I said as Grace, Lizzie, and I sat in her parlor drinking tea.

"No. No idea at all I'm afraid. Jeremiah has been to Port Huron to talk to the man in charge at the Army office, but he had no news to share either."

"I truly thought this would be over by now and that all the men would be home," said Lizzie, knitting her brow as she sipped the contents of her cup.

"I had Jeremiah give the Army office a letter I had written for David, but I have no idea if he will actually get it," said Grace wistfully.

"How are the children doing?" I asked.

"Jeremiah shows no emotion and neither does Arthur, but I find the girls crying quite often," replied Grace.

"Mariah has asked me to inquire as to how Jeremiah is faring. I feel she misses his visits and company," I said, taking a bite of the lovely biscuits that Grace had made.

"I am sure he does as well but there is simply too much to be done. He cannot spare the time, although I wish that he could. Perhaps Mariah could join us for supper one night this week?"

I nodded my approval. "Thank you, Grace. I will extend the offer to her, and I am sure she will welcome the chance to visit."

As I walked along the road home, I could not help but think that had David not volunteered it might be me and my children in Grace's place. The trees were in full leaf and the wildflowers had returned to adorn the roadway with their bright pinks and purples. Despite the beauty, my heart felt heavy, and a melancholy hung over me. I could see Charlotte tending to a flower garden on the side of the house and I walked up the path to say hello.

"Millicent!" she called out and waved as I got closer to the house.

"Good morning, Charlotte. I hope you don't mind my stopping by unannounced," I said as she smiled at me warmly.

"Of course not. Please come in," she said as she opened the garden gate. "Would you like some tea?"

"Oh, please do not go to any trouble," I replied.

"No trouble at all. Come in!" she said as she opened the

back door which led to the kitchen.

The kitchen was bright and sunny, and it still smelled of freshly hewn wood and bread freshly baked now sitting on the counter. A young girl who looked to be in her early twenties was washing dishes at the sink while a small brown dog lay on the floor near the stove, not even bothering to lift his head to make note of a stranger in its home.

"Brooke, could you bring us some tea and biscuits to the parlor please?" said Charlotte as she gestured toward a doorway.

"Of course, Mrs. Whitsitt," she replied with what was clearly a French accent.

I went through the doorway to a lovely parlor filled with very fine furnishings. There were not one but two leather and horsehair stuffed Chesterfields in a vibrant shade of rusty brown. Each was big enough to sit three people. A large exquisitely carved table sat between them holding a beautiful vase of flowers as well as a silver elephant and a few other trinkets, collected from their travels no doubt. It was an elegant room in every way with silk draperies on the windows and a portrait of a distinguished older man above the fireplace.

"Please, sit down Millicent," she said as she gestured to the sofa facing the window. She drew back the curtains to reveal a beautifully manicured garden and I could see a man trimming and clearing. I felt overwhelmed by the opulence of this house. Matthew's family home had been, I thought, quite grand but even it paled in comparison to the home I now found myself sitting in.

"Thank you, Brooke," she said to the girl as she set a tray with sweets, small sandwiches, and tea on the table. I have no idea how she prepared it so quickly. Perhaps others were working in the kitchen as well.

"Brooke is an unusual name," I said as I smiled at her.

"It is, as you say a nickname," she responded politely before heading back to the kitchen.

Charlotte poured me a cup of tea and used a pair of silver tongs to fill a plate for me.

"Our daughter gave her that nickname. She had trouble with her true given name, and we have kept it," said Charlotte as she handed the plate to me.

"I'm sorry, I didn't..." I stammered.

"Oh, my dear you need not worry. My heart, while still tender from loss, is not so fragile that it will break at the mere mention of my daughter," she replied, sipping from her cup.

"Your home is very beautiful," I said changing the subject.

"Thank you, we have been very fortunate to have so

many wonderful carpenters and craftsmen to help us in this endeavor. We are quite pleased by the result."

"And your husband?"

Charlotte put down her teacup, glanced up at the portrait on the wall, and sighed.

"Leo is very happy with the house of course but he stays upstairs mostly, as he has some difficulty walking now," she said candidly.

"I'm sorry Charlotte. I did not mean to pry," I said suddenly wishing I had stayed on the road to my own house.

"You are not. I have no secrets and I am sure people are wondering why they have not seen my husband in town. He has been unwell for some time, which is why we moved here to the country. The doctors thought it might rejuvenate his health, but there has been no improvement yet."

"I am sorry. Please do let me know if there is anything we can help with. Matthew is very capable, and he can do nearly anything you might need," I said sincerely.

"Thank you, Millicent, we have been blessed to have good and reliable help and for that, I am most grateful. I will certainly not hesitate should there be something we need. Thank you for your kindness," Charlotte replied with a hint of wistfulness in her voice.

Assuming the man in the portrait was her husband Leo he

looked to be nearly twenty years older than her although I did not know her actual age. Based on conversations we had I would think she was only four or five years old than I am, but one can never be sure. We chatted about the weather, the house, and of course, the conflict. Time flew by. The clock on the mantel struck two and I realized that Matthew and the children did not know where I was.

"I should be going," I said as I wiped my face on the delicate napkin. "Thank you for the tea and delicious treats," I added, rising to my feet.

"You are welcome anytime my dear, truly," she said as she walked me to the front door.

The foyer was even more grand than the parlor and a large ornate staircase swirled up toward the second level until it curved out of sight. I could faintly hear coughing coming from somewhere above us. While it might seem that Charlotte had a wonderful life, it must be difficult to be here in this big house with no children and an ailing spouse. Money is not the salve for every wound it would seem, and I count my own blessings as I walk the short distance back to the house.

The summer brings no end to the conflict, as skirmishes break out in western Virginia and soon after, a full-scale battle in Big Bethel. As the battles rage on it is clear this is no longer a simple case of a few rebels, but it is quickly becoming a real war between North and South. The calls continue for more men, and I do not doubt that when the harvest is completed, Matthew will go as he had said. I try not to dwell on it, truly I do. But, despite my efforts to push it away, it consumes my thoughts each and every day. I find myself more and more often hiding tears from the children.

Word has finally come that David Morgan has been wounded and is being cared for in a hospital outside Philadelphia. The extent of his injuries is not fully known but we pray fervently that he will recover fully and return home soon. Mariah has been to the Morgan home several times for supper over the last month and she also has been visiting the Whitsitt couple at Charlotte's request. She thought Brooke could use some companionship from someone closer to her own age and she and Mariah have become fast friends. It does my heart good to see her building stronger relationships here. Hopefully, that will be enough to keep her here at home. I would not be surprised if Jeremiah were to propose soon. I still feel she should wait another year at least but if Matthew leaves, a tighter bond between our families may be a good thing.

The heat of July is full upon us, and it must surely be difficult for the men fighting in what now has truly become a full-scale war. There is a battle near Manassas, Virginia they are calling the Battle of Bull Run. The Union Army is being led by General McDowell who seemed at first to have the upper hand by pushing back the Confederates, but then reinforcements arrived. Sadly, the General and his troops had to make a hasty retreat to Washington and the battle was lost. It is beyond my comprehension how the Union is performing so poorly; many have underestimated the ferocity of the Southern soldiers and their commitment to their cause.

Michigan is calling up more and more men and forming new Calvary units every week it seems. Matthew has reaffirmed his intention to go after the harvest and he plans to join the 6th Michigan Calvary which is forming up to leave the first of November. They need blacksmiths, as all of the cavalry units do, and he will answer the call. He has been told to make sure his clothes are navy blue as some militia arriving in grey uniforms have been confused with enemy soldiers wearing the same colors. There have even been rumors that some soldiers, on each side, have been killed by their own men in the confusion on the battlefield, unable to tell friend from foe.

In town last week I stood in line at Cook's with several other women buying navy wool cloth and brass buttons with which to make a uniform. The government has not been able to respond fast enough to the growing demand and it falls to individual soldiers to supply their clothing, at least for now. One by one I glanced at their faces as we waited. Each woman was possessed of the same blank stare people often have when they are facing an uncertain future. No one talked, no one smiled. Simple nods to acknowledge each other were the only greeting. But still, there was an unspoken sense of camaraderie, of shared pain… and fear. Would it be me? Would it be her? Which one of us would have her life changed forever?

I saw Brooke in town running errands for Charlotte. If I had known she was coming, we could have shared a wagon. I'll have to let Charlotte know in the future. There seems to be so much to do, and so many plans to make to be ready for when the time comes, but I can barely get through these conversations with Matthew without bursting into tears. It has become a source of terrible angst for him, seeing how much I already grieve and yet needing to be true to his convictions. I admire him, but at the same time how we will manage I do not really know. There is no possibility that the children and I can till and plant the acreage and we have no neighbors who can lend a hand. David has still not returned; Leo is unable to be of help and everyone has their own farms to care for.

We can maintain the garden for food, but we can't possibly plant for sale, so we have very limited ways to generate money. Matthew will be paid by the Army, but it is unclear how he might get those wages to us, if at all. The number of coins in the box seems to keep getting smaller and smaller as we spend for the things he will need, but we have no choice. On a hopeful note, Star and Moon have produced another foal and we can sell her to make some additional money. There is also another calf, making our herd six in total, and we could probably manage with one less. We will keep one bull calf and sell off the other. We will find a way, we always have… and God willing, we always will.

Kenneth is doing the best he can for a boy of twelve to learn from his father. He has taken on more and more of the daily chores. I do not think we will be able to spare him for school again in the fall so he may have to make do with the education he has. He is still such a very quiet boy, very meek, seldom complaining. Like Cordelia, he is very fearful of Rebecca whom he refers to as Rotten Rebecca, but never within her earshot. He has grown a bit this summer and he is as tall as Mariah which will be helpful when it comes to hitching the horses. All the children know that their father will be leaving in a few weeks, but he is the only one who never asks any questions or speaks of it.

Cordelia is the most curious, wanting to know what her father will be doing and where he will be going. She doesn't really understand the gravity of it but rather she sees it as an adventure he is embarking on, without the specter of possibly never returning. Mariah, of course, knows that is a possibility and she has shared in the pain that Jeremiah has felt about his own father. She has been very helpful of late, showering her father with affection which I know he relishes. Rebecca does not grasp the situation fully, but she does know that her father is going away. Charles, bless this little boy, my baby. He turned five this summer and truly does not understand what is happening. He senses that there is a sadness in me, and he often tells me to be more cheerful.

"Show me your smile Mama," he said, as he pulled up playfully on the corners of my mouth.

"I have a big smile," he added, sticking his hands in his mouth, and pulling his lips back as he bared all his teeth before falling into fits of laughter.

He is a sweet boy, with his father's eyes. His laugh reminds me of my dear mother's laugh, gone now over a year. I wonder how much of his father he will remember as the days pass. My prayer is that the days are short. That his father, my husband, returns quickly, and that life continues its current path.

The air is beginning to change. You can smell the dust and dirt on the breeze that is kicked up as the crops are brought down. It blows across the field toward the house, leaving a dusty film on every surface. The leaves on the trees are changing as the forest puts on its finest cloak of crimson and gold that sparkles in the sunlight. This is usually my favorite time of year. The days can be unexpectedly warm, but the nights are cool and crisp and the smell of logs burning fills the air. I love to walk through the forest as the leaves begin to fall, making a carpet beneath my feet. But not this year. These changes signal that the time is drawing near, the time for my world to change. As I stand on the back porch looking out into the now bare fields, I can feel the wave of sadness coming once again to drown me in sorrow.

"What are you doing my dearest?" asked Matthew as he came out of the house behind me.

"Nothing, just enjoying the evening air," I said as I leaned my back against him, his arms wrapped around me, his face next to mine as we gazed out on the setting sun.

"I know you are sad, and I know you are frightened, but you must trust in me, and you must trust in God. I will return to you and our children," he said quietly.

"You know I could not believe in you more, and with

every fiber of my being. I want to trust that all will be well, but there is so much we can't control or predict," I replied matter-of-factly.

Matthew turned me around to look at him, brushing the stray strands of hair out of my face.

"Millicent, I could not love you more. You have been a true wife and mother to our children and if I must crawl back to you on my hands and knees, then that is what I will do," he said as he kissed me deeply.

I breathed him in as if I could somehow capture his essence and this moment to keep with me when he was gone. We stood for a few minutes more on the porch before he led me inside to our room, locking the door behind him. The rising moon illuminated our room as we reveled the whole night in the closeness of each other, the pleasure of each other's arms. I could not remember a night of such intimacy and love, and I knew it would sustain me for the many lonely nights to come. I'm not sure when I fell asleep, but when I woke in the morning the sun was high in the sky, and Matthew was gone. I lie here for just another moment, relishing the warmth of the sheets and his scent all around me, when on his pillow I spied a flower from the garden left there for me. A beautiful red button of a flower that smelled of fall and spice. I put it in the glass I kept on the nightstand with a bit of water. It made me smile. But sadly, I must leave this room and face reality once again. There is still much to do.

Mariah and I bake biscuits and wrap up dried meat for Matthew to take with him. He will be riding Star, leaving Moon behind with her foal. She is a beautiful creature the children have named Tootie. All day he has been carefully packing his things and bed roll into saddlebags. Star seems to sense that he is leaving too as he struggles to be still while Matthew checks his hooves.

David Morgan returned a few days ago. Matthew and I were able to visit him and gather some helpful information about conditions on the battlefield. His injuries are still healing, and he walks with a stick, but he is hopeful for a full recovery. The stories he had to share from his experience, however, did nothing to quell the turmoil in my belly.

"We often did not have shelter or food to speak of, but things did improve a little as the weeks went by. When we did get paid, which was sporadic, we were often forced to use those monies to buy food in the towns and villages we were passing through," he said as Grace adjusted the blanket covering his legs.

"Was there a way to get money home?" asked Matthew as he glanced over at me.

"You can ask the paymaster to set aside some of your wages and he will transfer it to the office in Port Huron. But it does take time and honestly, you will need every penny you get for your own survival."

Matthew was clearly panicked by this news, not anticipating that he might not be able to have money to spare to send to us.

"Were you able to get mail?" I asked.

"Yes, thankfully. The Army set up wagons to serve as makeshift post offices. We could send and receive mail through them. Although it was slow, I did get letters from Grace and I was able to get letters to her from Philadelphia," he said, groaning slightly.

"David, you need to rest now," said Grace looking at us both.

"Of course," I said as I rose and bid David goodbye.

"I will join you in a moment. I want to speak to David privately for a moment," replied Matthew.

Grace and I retreated to the kitchen, and she hugged me tightly.

"I know you are frightened, and we are here for you and the children. Whatever you might need," she said.

"Thank you. I know that you are, and it is most appreciated," I replied.

"Jeremiah would like to speak to Matthew before he goes. I am sure you can guess why," she added.

I smiled at her, "Yes, I can. I am confident that Matthew will approve, although perhaps not right away. An engagement of six months or so might be best."

"We are in agreement. David and I are very excited to have Mariah join our family," she said hugging me again.

As I expected, Matthew did give his permission to Jeremiah to propose with the condition that they wait to marry until the spring, with the hope he would be here for it. Now it was up to Jeremiah to find the right time to ask her and for her to say yes. I was not sure what Mariah's opinion was on this matter as she never seemed to want to talk to me about it. I know the reluctance of girls to discuss some things with their mothers. I felt the same way when I met Matthew. She is certainly fond of Jeremiah, but was she interested in marrying him? I am not sure.

The remaining time passed quickly and before I could even blink, it was time for Matthew to leave to join up with the others in Port Huron. We had said our goodbyes last night in private. There were some things best not said in front of the children, like what we should do if he does not return. He took each child in turn into the parlor and spoke with them for a few moments before we all gathered in the kitchen.

"Now I must go. Remember what I have said to each of you today and do your best to be good and responsible for your mother. I hope to be back soon, but until I return, know that I will keep you all close to my heart and in my prayers," he said fighting back the tears.

With that, he kissed me one more time and then he was gone. I could not bear to go out to see him ride away. Instead, I sat with the children in the parlor and read to them from their favorite book *Two Doves and an Owl*. I could hear Star whinny as he went past the house as if he too was saying his goodbyes. I tried but I couldn't help myself. I ran to the front window and looked out. Matthew had stopped at the road and turned back to look at the house. Maybe he wouldn't go. Maybe he would change his mind. I held my breath. He could see me I was sure, and he hesitated for a moment before he tipped his hat to me, then turned and rode away.

"Mama, read more of the story please," said Kenneth, his voice cracking.

"Yes, please, Mama," chimed in Cordelia.

I sat back down in the chair and the children moved in a bit closer while I opened the book and found the place I had left off. I cleared my throat and began to read again.

"These little doves one spring had a nest and four young

ones. How very happy were they in feeding their little birds. The whole day they were busy, from the morning to the evening, carrying food and water to the nest. But one day the father of these little doves was obliged to go away a great distance and was gone the whole day. During his absence, a great Owl came and… "

I looked up at the children and I could see they were each wiping away tears. I had tried to contain mine, but I could hold back the torrent no more. The tears began streaming down my face, my body racked with sobs. I knew I should not be crying so in front of the children, but I could not hold it in, nor could they. Soon all we could do was huddle together and cry.

Chapter Five – *Alone*

The winter is cold and foreboding. The skies are dark and cloudy as if they are reflecting my very soul back to me. These dreary days make the work even more grueling, and I fall into bed each night exhausted from the effort of taking care of the family. It is good that I am so tired at night as otherwise I would not be able to sleep. The bed feels cold and lonely without Matthew in it. He has been gone for nearly three months now and I received my first letter from him just yesterday. I held it in my hands feeling the texture of the paper, smelling it to see if I could find his scent. To know that just a couple of weeks ago he held this paper in his own hands as I do now was a comfort. I read it over and over again until I could practically recite it by heart.

January 1862

My dearest,

We have been on the move now for many weeks, but the progress is slow as we move south to join other regiments in Kentucky. The roads have been difficult because of the rain or snow and the journey is slow. We have no tents to sleep in and I wake often cold and wet. Lately some of the other men and I have made a tarp of sorts with sticks and a blanket we found in a barn. Three of us have been able to huddle beneath it and that has been most helpful. Private William Roder, Private James Johnson, and I have become fast friends. We look out for each other as best we can.

We have seen no fighting yet but I've no doubt that will change soon and we have passed returning troops who have seen battle, lame and wounded as they retreat to the rear.

I have not been paid yet, but I hope that it will come soon. I will do my best to try and get some of it to you. My heart is often heavy thinking of the burden I have left you with, but I know you are strong and that our children are safe in your care. Please kiss them each for me and know that I miss you most ardently.

Your loving husband,

Matthew

My hands shook as I read the letter and my heart broke thinking of Matthew sleeping on the cold wet ground as I lay in our bed, my only complaint being that I sleep without him. Perhaps it was best if I did not read the letters to the children but rather just provided them with the news that their father was well and getting on. It was too much for them to also share my burden of guilt for our comfort while he suffered so.

Jeremiah has proposed to Mariah, but she has told him

she would like to wait until her father returns before becoming engaged. I was surprised by that response, but Jeremiah seemed to accept it and interpreted it as an agreement to marry, even though she had not actually said yes. She and Brooke see each other every week or so, she often comes to our home during her time off to talk and laugh with Mariah about the things young ladies of that age seem to talk about; mainly men and the fashion of the day. Brooke has brought some French magazines and Mariah looks through them voraciously, squealing over the fluffy pink confections that are often featured on their pages. Paris is a very far cry from the dreary drabness of our winter.

I am glad she has found a friend in Brooke. Although she is a few years older, she is able to be more of a friend to Mariah than the other girls nearby who are closer to Cordelia's age. My only concern is that spending time at Charlotte's magnificent home may cause feelings of dissatisfaction to rise within her compared to our life and what we have… or more accurately don't have. Even I have found it difficult at times not to be envious of the life that Charlotte leads, but then I remind myself that while financially safe, it is a lonely life it seems. Still, at this moment the security that comes with means would be most welcome. We will manage, but it will certainly not be easy. It occurs to me that life is seldom easy really. There is always some challenge or another that must be overcome. I think it must be God's way of making sure we do not become complacent in our devotion, always needing to turn to Him for help and healing.

February has been especially cold, and I will be grateful when the month is over, and we can start to anticipate the thawing of spring. I write to Matthew every week, but I've had no letters from him in a month. There was a battle in Mill Springs, Kentucky a few weeks ago and I can only assume that Matthew and his regiment were involved, but I have no direct knowledge other than what comes in the paper. Charlotte has demonstrated great kindness toward us by making sure I have the paper every Friday to keep abreast of what is happening. She has also sent over bread, cheese, and sweets whenever Brooke comes to spend time with Mariah. I can truly not thank her enough for these considerations, as they have made life a bit easier.

"Mariah, what are you reading?" I asked as I walked into her room with my arms full of clean clothes. She was peering intently at a piece of paper and did not seem to hear me when I entered.

Startled she looked up at me as she stammered a reply, "It's - It's nothing, Mother. It's just a poem. Yes, a poem, that

Brooke asked me to read."

I looked at her quizzically, her face flushing apple-red as she smiled at me.

"Oh, I see. Well, I would like to read it," I replied.

"She would not appreciate that, Mother. She shared it with me for my opinion of what she had written, and she asked me not to share it," she said firmly.

"I understand," I nodded as I turned to go back to the kitchen.

Young girls can be so secretive. I suppose it gives them a sense of control over their lives when truly they have little. I gave it no more consideration as preparations for supper took over my thoughts and kept me busy until it was time for bed. Just as I was about to drift off to sleep, I thought I heard a noise from the parlor. Charles, probably, or one of the other children no doubt, but I got up anyway to see for myself. The room was very cold, and I wrapped a shawl around my shoulders as I lit the oil lamp. I opened the door to the children's room, held up the lantern, and peered inside. I could see every bed filled and all was quiet and as it should be.

I slowly closed the door so as to not wake anyone and padded out into the parlor, which is where I thought the noise came from. I saw nothing. A search of the whole house turned up no source for what I had heard and so I went back to bed thinking it must have been in my mind. I slept fitfully with a gnawing sense that something was not right. Perhaps I would see more in the light of day.

I rose at dawn and dressed in layers to stave off the cold as I headed out to the barn to milk the cows. My fingers were cold and I held them close to the glass of the lantern trying to warm them.

"I am sorry, my dear," I murmured as I rubbed my hands together before reaching for her teats. "I know you dislike it when my hands are cold."

I was rewarded for my efforts with a low moo and the stomping of a hoof but other than that she did not protest. I enjoyed milking, truth be told, and I rested my cheek against the soft rotund belly of Susie, our Herford. I sat in silence going about the task when I heard the barn door creak behind me.

"Kenneth, what are you doing out here? You're not even dressed," I said as he came through the door.

"I'm hungry, Mama," he said rubbing his eyes sleepily.

"Tell Mariah to get up and make you some breakfast my dear."

"I tried to Mama, but she wasn't in her bed. It was just full of pillows under the blanket," he said shrugging his shoulders.

"She must be in the privy Kenneth. Go wait in the house," I replied.

"I knocked on the door, and when no one answered I opened it, but she wasn't there," he replied with a whine.

"All right. I'm nearly finished here. Go back in the house. I will be right there. Your sister is probably hiding to play a game with you," I said as I wiped my hands on my apron. I let the cow back into the pasture and carried the bucket of milk up to the house.

Cordelia and Rebecca were in the kitchen doing their best to make breakfast.

"Where is Mariah?" I demanded.

"She's not here Mama. We thought she was with you in the barn," replied Rebecca.

"Mariah!" I called out loudly but there was no reply. "Come out at once, Mariah. This is not a game I am playing."

But there was no reply. I began searching through the house, but she was nowhere to be found. I checked the privy myself and Kenneth was right… she was not there. The gnawing feeling I had during the night was now turning into a true panic. Where is Mariah? There had been a light dusting of snow last night and I could see only my footprints going from the house to the barn, so where else could she be? I walked around to the front of the house and noticed two sets of footprints, one leading up to the door, and two going away. I followed them out to the road where it was clear they had gotten onto a wagon or carriage. The noise I heard last night must have been from the front door. Suddenly the situation became clear. Mariah had run away.

I ran back into the house and went immediately to her bed where I could see that pillows and a shirt filled with straw had been laid out to make it look like someone was in the bed when covered with the blanket. Under her bed, the boxes that held her clothes and shoes were empty. Everything was gone.

I gathered the children together in the kitchen.

"Do any of you know where Mariah has gone and with whom?"

They all looked at me with blank stares. Clearly, they knew nothing. If Mariah had a plan, which it appears she did, she had not shared it with any of her siblings.

"Mama, I'm still hungry," said Kenneth looking close to tears.

"Of course, my darling," I said apologetically as I hugged him. "Rebecca, help me with breakfast please," I asked as I quickly set about getting hot cakes and bacon on the table for the children and a pot of coffee for myself. I usually had tea but today I was sure the coffee would be more necessary.

"Kenneth, I need you to watch your sister and brother while I go to see Mrs. Whitsitt," I said putting down my coffee cup.

"I can watch them, Mother," replied Rebecca.

Cordelia began to cry. The thought of being left alone with her sister was still terrifying to her.

"No Rebecca, I need you to come with me. Your brother can manage it can't you, Kenneth?"

"Yes Mama," he replied as he comforted Cordelia.

"Good boy," I said as I kissed him on the top of his head.

"Rebecca, get your coat. We need to go now," I said as I wrapped my scarf around my head. We quickly went out the door and headed to the Whitsitt home.

I stomped my feet to try and stay warm while we waited on the stoop for someone to answer. It seemed like an eternity before Mr. Fuller answered the door. I had met him before. He was a servant and caretaker and seemed like a kind man.

"Mrs. Wagner, good morning. Come in please as it's quite cold this morning," he said as he opened the door wide.

Rebecca's mouth gaped open as she gazed around at the splendor. She had never seen anything quite like it, but this was not a social call.

"Millicent, good morning," said Charlotte as she joined us

in the foyer. "Who is this with you?"

"Good morning. This is my daughter, Rebecca," I replied.

"It's nice to meet you, Rebecca. Come in, both of you," she said as she gestured toward the parlor.

"I'm sorry Charlotte but I can't stay. I need to speak to Brooke. Is she here?"

"Brooke?"

"Yes. Mariah is… gone," I said flatly. "I am hoping Brooke may know where she might be."

"Of course. Come into the parlor. Fuller, get Brooke at once."

"Thank you," I said following her to the parlor and continuing to hold on to Rebecca's hand, lest she begin touching things which she always likes to do.

"Sit here Rebecca and be quiet for Mama. Can you do that?" I asked as I put her in a big overstuffed blue chair.

"Yes, Mama, I can do that," she said as she ran her hands back and forth over the velvet, admiring its softness.

"No touching," I leaned over and whispered before turning to Brooke who had just joined us.

"Mrs. Wagner, Fuller says that you need to speak to me?" she said in that lilting French accent of hers. It sounded so calm and innocent, but I was sure she knew something.

"Yes, Brooke. I am wondering if you know where Mariah

has gone. She is not at our house," I said expectantly.

"If you know something Brooke, you must tell us at once," added Charlotte sternly.

"Mrs. Whitsitt, Mrs. Wagner I do not know where Mariah is. You say she is not at your home?" she said shaking her head.

"No, no she is not, and it appears that someone was at our house during the night and that she left with them, perhaps in a carriage or wagon. You know nothing of what she had planned or where she might have gone?"

I could see a realization dawning as Brooke looked back and forth between Charlotte and me.

"Oh, mon Dieu, qu'ai-je fait, mon Dieu," she replied, her voice cracking and nervous.

"English, my dear," reprimanded Charlotte.

"Oh, Mrs. Wagner I am sorry. I did not know this was what they had planned. I thought they were just talking, a flirtation you know…" she replied, her voice trailing off.

"Brooke, tell us all at once!" said Charlotte angrily.

"Who was Mariah engaging with?" I asked.

"John, John Parker. They were writing to each other. I would carry the letters back and forth for them, it has been so for several months now. But truly Madame I did not think that anything would come of it, certainly not this," she said as she looked at me despondently.

"Oh, Brooke why would you have done such a thing? You should have spoken to me before agreeing to do this for Mariah," said Charlotte wringing her hands in dismay.

"My apologies Madame, I thought I was helping a friend. I did not know this is where it would lead."

"Brooke, do you know where they have gone?" I said at last.

"No, Madame, I do not but one can only assume that they have gone to the inn which the Parker's own," she replied flatly.

"You must go at once, Millicent. I will have Fuller take you in the carriage."

"But the children?"

"Do not worry about the children. I will have Brooke bring them here and we will feed them and care for them till you return," she replied.

I glanced over at Rebecca, she was still rubbing her hands back and forth on the chair, petting it almost as if it were an animal. My heart raced at the thought of the damage she could do if left unattended in this house.

"Charlotte, your offer is very generous, but Rebecca…" I replied as my voice trailed off.

"Say no more. I understand," she said confidently. "My

sister was very much like Rebecca I suspect, and I know that she will need extra care."

I breathed a sigh of relief. At least I did not have to try and explain Rebecca to Charlotte, as that would not be quick or easy. Now I could turn my attention to Mariah.

"So, it is settled. Fuller, get the carriage at once and take Mrs. Wagner wherever she needs to go. Millicent, I will get you a heavier coat, and there are furs in the carriage to keep you warm. Do not worry about the children. Do what you must to find your daughter," Charlotte said as she hugged me tightly.

"I cannot thank you enough. You are a dear friend, truly," I said as I choked back tears.

It seemed as if the ride into town took much longer than usual but Fuller was driving the horses as fast as he could. The road was bumpy but dry. I had never seen the inn on the south side of town but Fuller knew of the place. I did not ask him how as I did not want to know. The sun was high in the sky when we finally arrived and I was impressed with what I saw. The building was entirely made of brick and stone in a very ornate style with a wide drive that could accommodate carriages on both sides. I could see at least four chimneys, each one spewing gray smoke into the air. On the side of the building was a trellis which looked like it led to a garden with a gazebo. I'm sure was stunning in the spring. Two men were standing outside the door dressed nicely in heavy coats and top hats, but I was not sure if their job was to keep people out, or in.

"Mrs. Wagner, why don't you wait here for a moment," said Fuller as he tied the carriage up to one of the many iron stanchions.

I nodded. Honestly, now that we had arrived, I did not even know what I would say to her, assuming of course she was here. And what if she were not? If she were with John Parker, there is no guarantee that they would come here. They could have gone anywhere. If Matthew were here, he would know what to do and what to say to her. But he is not here, and so I must find my own words.

I watched while Fuller spoke to one of the men. The other opened the door and let a man in who had just arrived on horseback. The man had pulled his hat down over his eyes and did not look in my direction before slipping inside. I did however recognize the horse as one I had seen Mr. Hanson from the bank riding. I wanted to laugh out loud at the absurdity of his attempt to hide himself from me when his horse might have just as well announced his name for all to hear.

"Mrs. Wagner, it appears that Mariah is in fact here. She

arrived with Mr. Parker earlier this morning according to the man here that I spoke with," said Fuller as he stood next to the carriage.

"He told you that?"

"Yes, ma'am. It took some coaxing and a couple of coins, but he did confess to me that your daughter is here."

"Oh, Fuller you must let me repay you when we return home," I said at once.

"No need Mrs. Wagner. Mrs. Whitsitt gave me money for this very purpose, and you need not worry about that."

One more thing to be grateful to Charlotte for. I was going to be deeply in her debt when this was over, it was clear.

"What would like you to do ma'am?" asked Fuller.

"Will he let me in?" I asked.

"Yes, is that what you would like to do?"

I nodded. I had come this far, and no matter what it takes I must speak to Mariah, and she must return home with me. Fuller helped me from the carriage, and I was grateful for the warmth of the coat Charlotte had lent me. It also helped me to feel more grand and less intimidated by those I was undoubtedly going to meet inside. As Fuller had said, the man he had spoken to opened the door letting us in and closing it behind us with a large thud. The foyer was dimly lit and it took my eyes a minute to adjust. The walls were covered with a red and black printed fabric and there were two staircases, one on either side, made of brass and wood. The rug was thick, as plush as any I had ever seen, and it had large tassels on each end made of gold thread that sparkled. There was a large clock with a pendulum in one corner of the foyer and an ornate desk at which sat an impeccably dressed and coifed young woman. The air smelled of perfume and lamp oil.

There were several large doors, all closed, but I could hear both men's and women's voices coming from behind one of them. The young woman looked at me calmly as if seeing a woman come to this place was an everyday occurrence. I sincerely doubted that it was.

"How may I help you?" she said in measured and precise tones.

"I'd like to speak to John Parker," I said just as calmly.

"Is Mr. Parker expecting you?" she asked.

"No, I am sure he is not, but I am also sure he will speak to me when he learns that I am here," I replied.

Fuller stepped up to the desk and leaned in whispering something in her ear and placing something in her hand. More money I was sure, but I could not dwell on it now.

"You may wait in here," she said as she rose opening one

of the doors which led to a small drawing room.

"Thank you," I said as she quietly closed the doors behind us. The room was decorated in the same colors and fabric as the foyer but also contained two large settees that were upholstered in heavy gold fabric that adorned frames and legs of ornately carved wood. I wondered if I dared sit down, but it felt like the polite thing to do. Fuller stood close by for which I was very grateful. His presence was reassuring, and he seemed confident and capable. I suppose he has seen many kinds of situations with the Whitsitt family given their worldwide travels, although I was sure not one such as this.

The fire in the grate offered a welcome warmth as the clock on the mantel ticked away the minutes, which soon became an hour. What if he wasn't coming after all? What would I do then? Fuller must have read my mind.

"Be patient, ma'am. If he does not come soon, we will try a different tactic."

Another twenty minutes passed before a small door in the back of the room opened and through it came John Parker at last.

"Mrs. Wagner, it's a pleasure to see you again, but I must say this is highly unusual. What can I do for you?" he asked smiling as though he had no idea why I was here.

"Mariah is here?"

"Yes, she is, but she has no desire to see you," he replied calmly.

I could feel the redness rising in my cheeks and I appreciated the calming touch of Fuller's hand on my shoulder.

"I am her mother, and I demand to see her, now," I said firmly.

John smiled as he crossed his arms across his chest and leaned back on the settee. He studied my face as if wondering how vehemently I was going to insist. Would I make a fuss, scream even? He could not be sure, and my face revealed nothing to him of what I was thinking.

"Mrs. Wagner, I know this must be difficult, but I love Mariah, and she loves me. She is going to be my wife. I will not make her do something she does not want to do," he said finally.

"Mr. Parker, I think it would be in your best interest to let Mrs. Wagner see her daughter. Otherwise, we will have to return here with the Deputy Constable to ensure that Miss Wagner has not been brought here against her will. I doubt very much your guests would appreciate his presence here," he added.

I looked up at Fuller appreciatively. That was an approach I had not considered. John sat there for another minute contemplating his next move.

"I will bring her down in a moment. If you will excuse me," he replied.

It was indeed only a few minutes before he returned with Mariah. I almost didn't recognize her. Her hair had been curled and she was wearing a dress of fine embordered silk in a dark blue color which complemented her skin.

"Mariah," I said as I stood to embrace her.

"No, Mother. Please don't," she said raising her hand.

Shocked, I sat back down on the settee.

"I'd like to talk to my daughter alone, if I may," I said quietly.

"Of course," said John as he ushered Fuller into the other room.

"Mother, before you say anything, let me speak," said Mariah as soon as the door closed behind them.

I waited expectantly but apprehensively as Mariah sat down across from me, smoothing her fancy dress as she did. This could not be my daughter… the girl who slept in my home just last night. She seemed so different, so distant.

"I want to say, Mother, that I am sorry that I left without saying goodbye. I knew that you would try to stop me. I love John and we are going to be married. He is offering me a better life, a life where I do not have to work so hard and take care of others. Instead, I can have others to look after me," she said.

"But Mariah at what cost does this better life come? You will forever be associated with this house of ill repute and you and your children will be tarnished by that forever. Is that what you want?"

"No, it is not, but if that is the price that must be paid for a better life, then so be it. Others can judge me if they wish but I will be living in this house and wearing these clothes while others live like-"

"Live like our family?" I interjected.

"Yes, Mama, like our family. You do not even know how you will manage now that father is gone, and who knows if he will return," she replied.

"Mariah don't say that! You know that your father will return, and he is doing what he believes is right, what is honorable. Perhaps you don't understand that kind of character."

"I understand that you will have one less mouth to feed and for that, you should be grateful," she retorted.

"Mariah, I barely recognize you as my daughter. I don't know how you can say these things. What would your father think if he could see you right now?" I asked wearily.

"He would see someone who is taking control of their

life to make things better for themselves. Isn't that exactly what he is doing? Fighting to give slaves a better life in the South? Perhaps before he did that, he should have thought about giving us a better life here. But since he did not, I will fight for myself. Now I must go, Mother. Go home," she said as she rose and went back out through the small door.

I sat in stunned silence. The audacity of it, the selfishness. How could this possibly be my daughter? Matthew would be furious. He would take her by the arm and drag her home if need be. But if I did that, how long would she stay before she ran away again? She wants to take the easy way out of what she sees as an unhappy life of hard work and honest living. Sadly, it seems that I have no choice but to let her.

Chapter Six - *These Daughters of Mine*

April 1862

My dearest,

*I*t *pains me so to hear that Mariah has chosen the path of impropriety and wealth over a life of good character. We raised her with good Christian values, and I do not understand how she could do this. But we must not dwell on it. She is grown now and can make her own way as she chooses.*

My concern is how you will manage now. Rebecca cannot be relied upon for things beyond simple repetitive tasks and she can clearly not be trusted to watch the littles. I know you said that Grace and Jeremiah are not speaking to you, but you are blameless in this. David had agreed that Jeremiah could help you. Now, it seems that will not be the case.

If you must, sell one of the cows to provide money with which to purchase necessities. I have asked the paymaster to send you half of my wages from this month's pay, but many men warn that they are dishonest and that their families never receive the money. Still, I will try.

We are riding toward Tennessee to a place called Shiloh where General Grant intends to battle against the Confederates. Many are ill with dysentery, which runs through the camps where conditions are often very poor and contain tainted water. I shot a wild turkey yesterday and William, James, and I ate heartily for a change. We were on watch away from the main campsite, which was a blessing in this case. This was the first meat we had eaten in many days. The weather is rainy, and we continue to try to find ways to stay dry, but it is never easy, and the constant wetness of our clothes makes for very cold nights. Our hope is as the days get warmer, they will at least dry in the light of day. We work all day to gather wood, build fires, groom the horses, and check their shoes. It is trying, and despite the cold and wet, we fall asleep instantly when we are not on watch.

My heart yearns for you, and my arms long to hold you. I hope I will be home soon. Kiss the children for me.

Your loving husband,

Matthew

The paper brings news of the marriage of John Parker and Mariah Wagner in Port Huron this week and now my shame is complete. The entire community is aware of my daughter's choice. Already neighbors have stopped calling on us or taking our visits, everyone really, except Charlotte. She feels great guilt for the part Brooke played in what has happened, although I do not blame her at all. Her friendship and support during these trying times have meant more than she could know. Fuller has come to plant a few acres of hay so that we will have what we need for the animals, and he helped to prepare the garden as well. Rebecca, Cordelia, and I will plant corn, beans, squash, carrots, onions, and some herbs. We also have a small patch of wheat we will use for flour. Milk from the cows and eggs from the hens will help, but I will need to set some traps at the edge of the forest to catch some rabbits, or better yet a deer. Charlotte sent us a ham and that has been most helpful, but it will not last much longer.

Each day after breakfast, Rebecca and I walk Cordelia, Kenneth, and Charles to school, so it is just the two of us during the day. The house seems quiet and empty without Mariah here. My feelings toward her are a mixture of anger and longing. No matter what she has done she is still my daughter and I miss her, but I know that I can never forgive her for what she has done to me and this family. These are the last months we can spare Kenneth and Cordelia for school. There is simply too much to be done around the farm, so when classes end in May it will be their last.

It has become a chore to ensure that Rebecca is not left with the littles, which means she must stay with me whenever I leave the house. But she is happy to visit Charlotte's and there is a small room off the kitchen that has been designated for her use when she is there. She will have something to eat and play with a doll or read a book. The respite from constantly being watchful over her is very welcome.

"How are you faring?" asked Charlotte as we sat down to tea in the parlor.

"As you would expect, I suppose," I replied mustering up a bit of a smile.

"What can I do for you my dear?" she asked as she took a bite of a small sandwich.

"Charlotte, you have done so much for me and my children already. I will never be able to repay you or thank you enough. Your kindness to Rebecca has been especially appreciated," I replied.

"My sister, Deborah, was very much like Rebecca. She was capable of some things but not others, and she was unpredictable, prone to outbursts of anger that seemed to bubble up from inside her for no reason."

"Where is your sister now?" I asked.

"My mother died three years ago; she was living with her until then. After she passed, Leo and I decided it would be good for her to be in a place where she could be cared for by those who knew best how to do so. She lives with the Daughters of Charity at a private mental hospital on Michigan Avenue in Detroit."

"I did not know such places existed," I replied

thoughtfully.

"There are few to be sure, but they care for her very well there and I visit a few times a year. She seems to be content," said Charlotte.

"How is Leo?" I asked. I have yet to see him, but the coughing persists from upstairs every visit.

"Unchanged, sadly. I do not see that this move has brought him any improvement, but it has certainly been good for me. I like the quiet of this place, the solitude… but do not think that means I do not enjoy your visits. I most certainly do," she said as she smiled at me.

We chatted all afternoon until it was time to retrieve the children from school, but Rebecca was very reluctant to leave and became most difficult. I practically had to drag her from Charlotte's home.

"I don't want to go," she said resisting my effort to take her hand.

"Rebecca we must go and fetch your brothers and sister. Now come along at once," I said, my hands on my hips, my brow knitted in consternation.

"No!" she said as she kicked me in the leg. The pain dropped me to my knees.

I grabbed at my shin. The pain coursing through my leg was intense and I feared it might be broken. Rebecca looked at me with surprise on her face.

"I didn't know I could make you fall," she said with surprise as she tried to help me up.

"Rebecca you are full-grown and very strong. You cannot lash out at people this way. You have hurt me most profoundly," I said as I fought back tears, struggling to get on my feet.

"Mrs. Wagner are you alright?" said Fuller as he and Brooke came running from the house, having seen our exchange.

"I'm not sure," I replied.

"Here, don't put any weight on it. Let me carry you," said Fuller as he scooped me up and carried me into the house.

Brooke took charge of Rebecca who was very happy, of course, to be going back into the house. Fuller set me on the Chesterfield facing the window in the parlor while Charlotte went to get some liniment. I pulled up my dress and pushed my stocking down to my ankle. My leg had developed a deep red spot as large as my hand and it was turning blue very quickly.

"I don't think it's broken," said Charlotte as she applied the liniment and bandaged my leg from my knee to my ankle. "But it is going to be quite painful for some time."

"I need to go. I have to collect the children from school,"

I said as I tried to get up from the sofa.

"I have already sent Brooke and Fuller to get them. I was not sure if they would go with him if he were alone, but I know they are familiar with Brooke. They will get them and bring them here. You rest for now. I have some laudanum for you," she said pouring from a dark glass bottle into a small spoon.

"But Rebecca, she should not be left alone to wander. She might break something," I said hesitating.

The pain in my leg was intense but I was reluctant to take the syrup she offered, knowing it would make me sleepy. How would I watch the children?

"I will keep an eye on Rebecca till Brooke returns. Millicent, I can see the very wheels turning inside your head. You and the children can stay here as long as you need. Fuller can tend to the cows and make sure things are secure at your home."

"Charlotte I can't, truly. You have been too kind."

"Enough, take this," she said insistently, sounding very much like my mother as she held the spoon up to my mouth.

I nodded reluctantly, opened my mouth, and took the medicine.

It was dark outside when I awoke, lying on a bed lightly covered with a blanket. Outside the window, I could see the tops of the trees in the light of the moon. I must be upstairs. My leg felt as if it were on fire and my head ached while my stomach growled. I turned and tried to sit up on the side of the bed but putting my leg down made it hurt even more and I quickly lay back down. This was a lovely room, decorated in pale blues and greens. Fuller must have carried me here but now I heard and saw no one save the ticking from a clock in the hallway. Should I call out? I did not want to disturb Leo if he were sleeping. There was no clock in my room so although it was dark, I did not know how late it truly was. Then I saw on the nightstand a small silver bell. I'd read in books how bells were used to call servants. Perhaps this was left here for that purpose. I picked it up and it made a small tinkling sound as I shook it gently, but I heard no response. Again, I shook the bell harder this time, and it rang out shrill and loud in the quiet.

"Mrs. Wagner, you are awake?" said a plump large-breasted woman, as she came into the room and lit the lamp.

She was wearing a white dress, an apron, and a small white cap. She appeared to be a nurse of some sort, presumably for Leo. I hoped she was not here just for me.

"How are you feeling my dearie?" she asked as she fluffed up the pillows behind me and straightened the blanket.

"You are?"

"Oh yes, my apologies ma'am. I'm Mrs. O'Connell I work for the Whitsitt's helping to care for Mr. Leo," she replied.

"Where are my children?" I asked anxiously.

"Rebecca is sleeping downstairs with Brooke so she can keep an eye on her, little rascal that she is. Kenneth and Charles are to your left, Cordelia to your right. They're all fed and sleeping soundly I should hope. I've heard nothing from the wee ones in a couple of hours. Ye need not worry dearie, we are taking good care of your clan," she added as she patted me on the arm.

"Thank you, Mrs. O'Connell, very much," I replied.

"Can I fetch you something to eat dearie?"

"No, I can go down to the kitchen," I said trying again to get up, but Mrs. O'Connell quickly intervened.

"Don't think that is wise lassie, take this offer while you have it. Let others take care of you for a change. I'll have Fuller bring a tray up for you."

As I lay here waiting for Fuller to come with something to eat, I began to recognize what had enticed Mariah to make the decision that she did. But still, the cost of that life was paid for with her honor, her very soul, and that was a price I would never pay. We stayed with Charlotte for a few days before Fuller took me home in the carriage. The children went on endlessly about how wonderful their visit was and while I had appreciated the care, I worried that the rest of my children had also now tasted a different life, one far and above what we had. Would that cause them to become less satisfied with what being on the farm could offer them? I hoped not.

The news of the war has been good of late with the Union prevailing at Shiloh and not long after in New Orleans, taking control of the mouth of the great river. I have not received any money from Matthew, and I will tell him to stop trying. It does not seem that the process works, or it is rife with corruption. Either way, he should keep the money for himself as we will manage. I did indeed sell one of the bulls as he had suggested, and he fetched a very good price. With that money, I bought a pig and some more chickens as well as sugar, tea, and flour. The rest of the money went into the box under the bed.

Going into Port Huron made me very nervous, but no one said anything unkind or treated me in a way that I felt was different, unlike my own community. Perhaps because the Parkers are contributors to the welfare of the town they are seen as less of the pariah that we see them as. I was also afraid of running into John, his aunt, or even Mariah as I did not know what I would say. I felt less confident without Fuller by my side. But there was a letter for me at the Army office which brightened my countenance greatly.

July 1862

My dearest,

I received your letter about the money, and I will do as you ask, although it increases my guilt as to the welfare of you and the children. I am glad you received a good price for the bull, and it seems as though you have made wise choices. It heartens me to know your leg has healed and that you are well.

William died yesterday of a gunshot wound he received a week ago. It festered and there was nothing more the doctor could do for him. I shall miss his company.

Every day is filled with drilling and practicing how to load our weapons. Day in and day out is much the same. The weather is intolerable now. The heat of summer has fully borne down on us now and this uniform, warm in the winter, is now suffocating and hot. The dust from the dry roads is often choking and covers us from head to toe. It is a relief when we can get into a river or stream and bathe and rinse off one set of clothes. We must wear them day after day. I was able to buy a second linen shirt and more paper, which has been a real luxury, but again this brings feelings of guilt as I know you do without so much on my behalf.

We are returning to Manassas, which is the same area the Army fought in about a year ago in the Battle of Bull Run. With God's grace, we will prevail this time. We cannot achieve real success in this war unless we can attack the enemy at their core. I now have Star hitched to a wagon that transports tack, blankets, and my shoeing supplies for the horses. It is a comfortable ride, but I fear it also makes me more of a target for the Confederates who often hide behind the trees and shoot at us as we make our way down the road. I have asked the captain for another soldier to ride with me but that has not happened yet. I will keep trying.

My love to you and the children, I will write again when I can.

Your loving husband,

Matthew

Sadly, Matthew's optimism was not warranted, and the Union was once again routed in the now-called Second Battle of Bull Run. Despite this defeat, there was much praise for the valor and distinction of a group called Meagher's Irish Brigade which included the 69th New York State Regiment. The larger scale battles were occurring now every few weeks and with that, the ever-mounting number of casualties. Mr. Wheeler from Wales was killed recently, and I heard his wife has since sold the farm and moved her and her children back in with her parents. The son of Mrs. Champlain was also killed. He was their only son and had yet to marry. Yet the summer marches on, not stopping to take note of the things that man wants or does. This has been a banner year for the garden, and we will have plenty to can for the larder. I may need to get some more jars.

The children find a way to enjoy a few days of fun at the pond, swimming and splashing about and just being children, which happens so seldom. Kenneth is showing Charles how to fish and the two of them laugh and carry on as boys do. It warms my heart to see. It is a true sadness that in Matthew's absence the children must do more of the work than they might have to do otherwise, but there is no alternative. I still try to do my best to be sure that they have moments when they can just be children, but it is true that there are many more moments when they are truly doing the work of grownups.

September 1862

I write this quickly as we are moving toward a place called Antietam where they say a very large battle is coming. Perhaps this will be what we need to end this war once and for all, and it is my daily prayer that it is over soon, and this loss of life can end. Lincoln signed the Confiscation Act which means we can more easily seize Confederate property and emancipate slaves who are in Union-occupied territory. This has allowed us to gather more supplies from the homes of

Confederate supporters. It also means escaped slaves do not have to be returned, and a small colored regiment is forming. They will fight alongside us.

Pray fervently for my safe return to you and know that my love for you is unbroken.

Your loving husband,

Matthew

The last few weeks have been the most trying in anticipation of this action which Matthew warned me about. Finally, news has come about a ferocious battle fought in Maryland in the place called Antietam. Many are calling it the bloodiest day of the war so far. Some say the Union lost nearly thirty thousand soldiers in just one day and General Lee, who led the Confederates, also suffered heavy losses on their side as well.

Every week I scour the newspaper for the names of the men who have been lost and captured, printed in long columns often filling a whole page as it includes the entire state of Michigan. Sometimes Army officers go to the home of soldiers who have been killed, but when there have been significant casualties, they simply can't keep up with the number of visits they must make. Each time I have been in Port Huron these past few months I see the lines of women waiting outside the Army office. Some are waiting to file for pensions, their husbands having died. Others are there to inquire of men who have been wounded or captured to see what their status might be.

The fall is now fully upon us. Kenneth seemed to accept my decision not to return him to school, although Cordelia was very disappointed. She would like to be a teacher and she knows that is not possible without continuing her own education. I will do the best I can to help her but there is a limit to my own knowledge, and she may already be brushing up against that. Perhaps Charlotte can provide some stimulation, as she is more worldly and educated than I am, but I hesitate to ask for anything more. She has already been so generous.

The garden has yielded a good crop and I work hard to harvest and preserve as much as I can to get us through the winter. Fuller has helped us to harvest the hay and the barn is full, adequately stocked for the winter. Kenneth has been a great help, and I can see him growing up before my very eyes, although I wish it had not happened so soon. It is too bad that the neighbors shun us as he has no boys his own age to socialize with. Fuller is the only man he has to talk to.

Cordelia has been sick of late, coughing and with little appetite. I am sure it is nothing more than that which seems to come every year at this time. But to be safe, I have moved her bed into my room to limit her exposure to the other children. Our family has been blessed with strong constitutions and the children have seldom been ill, and Matthew never, so I am not overly concerned. I've decided to make her favorite meal, a supper of chicken and carrots. Perhaps that will encourage her to eat. Just as I was about to set supper on the table there was a knock at the front door.

It was already dark, and I couldn't imagine who it may be. I was even more surprised to see Grace standing on the porch, David waiting in the carriage just beyond her, near the road.

"Grace, come in. Is everything alright?"

"No, it is not. I am sorry Millie, but we are on our way home from Port Huron. We felt we had to stop and show you the paper," she said as she handed it to me.

My heart leaped into my throat and my hand was shaking so much I could barely take the paper from her.

"Here, under captured," she said pointing to a section circled in pencil on the front page. *Sargent Matthew Wagner, Michigan 6th Calvary Company C.* There in black and white.

I could not speak. My breath felt like it would not come as I glanced from Grace to the paper in my hand, but the words did not change. They remained the same. Matthew had been captured by the enemy.

"Thank you," I said finally.

"There is something else, here," she said opening the front page and pointing to an article. "It's called The Preliminary Emancipation Proclamation which has been announced by President Lincoln. He has said that if the Confederates do not end the fighting and rejoin the Union by January 1st all slaves in rebellious states would be free."

I looked at her with shock. "Well surely the fighting will stop then, won't it?"

"I do not know. David does not think so, but we can be hopeful," she replied.

"Mama, we are waiting," yelled Rebecca from the kitchen.

"I have to feed the children, but thank you again, I appreciate you coming to tell me," I said quietly.

"I am sorry Millie, truly," she said before she turned and left joining David in the carriage, and I watched as they drove north toward their home. Her husband had come back to her. He is doing quite well by all accounts. I had to believe that Matthew would return to me, too.

I took a deep breath. I quickly decided not to share this with the children until I could learn more. I put the paper on the top shelf of the highboy for now.

"Who was at the door, Mama?" asked Kenneth as I began to set the plates on the table.

"Mrs. Morgan stopped by to give me some news from town."

"Is it about Mariah?" asked Rebecca hopefully.

"No, I'm afraid it is not. It was about another friend," I replied hoping they would not hear the fear in my voice. I forced myself to smile and talk to them as we ate as though nothing was wrong, but under the table, my legs were shaking. Cordelia did eat more than she had in some time and that reassured me, but during the night she coughed a great deal. No matter. I was not even trying to sleep but instead found myself pacing back and forth, stopping every few minutes to peer out the window. The moon was full and bright, a harvest moon they call it… orange and full in the sky just above the trees. The wind was blowing vigorously sending the leaves flying from the trees and scurrying across the dirt as if they were little mice. Christmas would be here in just a few weeks. It would be another Christmas without Matthew, and now without Mariah.

I read the paper over and over. Lincoln's plan to free the slaves surely would force the South to surrender. If the President freed all slaves, wouldn't they simply flee from the plantations? If that were to happen it seems the South would have nothing more to fight for. Slavery would be over. I could not pretend to understand their plight, their suffering, but I had to think this was good news for Matthew. If the war ends in just two months or so at the start of the new year, then he could be home in three months perhaps. Maybe he would even be safer in an enemy prison camp instead of on the battlefield. At least no one was shooting at him there. Conditions there couldn't be any worse than what he has endured under the Union Army, could they? I did not know. For now, I needed to focus on Cordelia who suddenly seemed to be getting worse.

Over the next two weeks, the doctor came several times, thanks to the coins in the box from the sale of the bull. But it was of no avail, and I could do nothing but watch as my daughter grew weaker and weaker, until she simply faded away. This was the second child I had lost to illness; our son Dickie had died when he was only four. Mariah and Rebecca would barely remember Dickie's passing. The others were too young, and Charles had not even been born yet. But this felt so much worse. Cordelia had been a smart, funny, and sensitive twelve-year-old just a few weeks ago. Now she lay in a wooden box in the parlor. Her brothers and sisters would feel this loss most devastatingly. What would Matthew think when he returned home to find another precious daughter lost, this time for good?

We would bury her in the Mt. Pleasant Cemetery next to Dickie. There was a place there for me and for Matthew, and with God's grace I knew I would see her again in heaven. Charles held tightly to my hand as Preacher Adams read out the scripture. Kenneth and Rebecca held on to each other in a rare moment of unity. Charlotte was there with Brooke, Fuller, and Mrs. O'Connell, which was much appreciated. Grace and Lizzie even came, setting aside for a moment any feelings of animosity they might have toward me. There were a few other families too, and the teacher from the school. They had all seen Cordelia grow up and I'm sure they had affection for her. How could they not?

As we were preparing to leave the cemetery, I saw a young woman dressed in black exit from a closed carriage and make her way to the grave now filled in with a golden pile of fresh dirt. I stopped to watch her. She laid a single flower on the dirt, then kissed her gloved fingers before touching them to the ground. As she returned to the carriage she stopped for a moment and looked my way. It was Mariah, who was clearly with child. She nodded in my direction, then climbed into the carriage and it drove away.

Chapter Seven - *Lost and Found*

November 17, 1862

Dear Mrs. Wagner,

We regret to inform you that your husband, Sgt. Matthew Wagner currently serving in the Michigan Calvary has been taken captive by Confederate forces. While he is a prisoner of war his wages will be held as credits by the US Army and will be issued to him upon his return.

Reports suggest that he is being held in a prison camp at Belle Isle, Virginia. There is no further status report as to his condition. You may communicate with your nearest Army office for additional reports as they become available.

Yours respectfully,

Lieutenant Arthur Wilson

Michigan Calvary Regiment Assistant Commander

The paper felt heavy in my hands. The ink was dark blue, or perhaps black. The handwriting was neat, with just one small ink splot near the word *yours*. It was obvious that the letter and the signature were from two different people. I'm sure Lieutenant Wilson would not have had time to write all the necessary letters himself. I wonder how many of these he had signed in the last few weeks to the wives and mothers of men both dead and captured. I knew the information it contained already, of course, because the reports in the newspaper were much faster than the Army. The task of writing and sending individual letters must be much more laborious.

The Battle of Antietam in Maryland was the bloodiest single day in the war so far, the papers had said. Twenty-three thousand men were killed, wounded, or missing. Some of the missing were deserters, while some were dead but with their bodies yet to be recovered. Others were captured by the Confederates, their fates uncertain. The number was hard to comprehend or picture in my mind. Had our fields held twenty-three thousand stalks of corn? Were there twenty-three thousand leaves on the large oak behind the house?

In homes all over the North, women like me sat holding these letters caring not as much about the many but grieving for the one most precious to her. A husband, a brother, a son, perhaps lost forever. I took some solace in knowing that Matthew was still alive. The worst had not happened yet. There was hope. There had to be hope, for without it I would surely die myself.

Rebecca has been unusually quiet since Cordelia died and she has cried very little. It is hard to know what the impact of this loss will be on my children; I know I carry the weight of it every day. Mariah, Matthew. Now Cordelia. My heart is so heavy I have moments when I feel like my heart is so full of pain that there is no room for joy. And, if a moment of joy does appear, I wipe it away, feeling such guilt as I think about what Matthew's life must be like. There have been periodic prisoner exchanges, and I am praying every day that Matthew will be released soon, either through exchange or the end of the war.

"Mama, can we chop down our Christmas tree today?" asked Charles as I was making breakfast.

My goodness. I had forgotten that the holiday would be upon us soon. I looked at his little upturned face and realized I needed to give my attention to those who are here and give my prayers to those who are not.

"Yes, my dear. I don't see why we could not do that. In fact, it's a good day. We should do it now before it gets too cold," I said trying to smile.

"Yeah!" shouted Charles as he ran several times around the table gleefully shouting and clapping his hands.

It was infectious and soon Kenneth and Rebecca joined in. When breakfast was cleared, we bundled up and traipsed across the field to the edge of the forest to search for a small tree.

"Charles, do not wander off on your own. Stay near to me or your brother or sister," I reminded him.

"I will, Mama," he reassured me.

We wandered around for a few minutes while inspecting various trees until Kenneth found the perfect little spruce.

"This one, this one!" he shouted out as he proudly showed off the tree he had chosen.

"Oh, wonderful my son, I think that is perfect. What do you say, Rebecca?"

I looked around but I did not see her.

"Rebecca!" I called out loudly.

There was no reply. Now Kenneth and Charles were calling out too and cries of "Rebecca!" filled the forest but there was no reply.

"Kenneth, do you know where you saw your sister last?"

"I'm sorry, Mama. I'm not sure. I was so busy looking at the trees I did not see where she went," he said sheepishly.

"Charles, did you see where sissy went?"

He started to cry and grabbed onto my coat wiping his face on my scarf. I picked him up and held him tightly.

"Not to worry my darling, not to worry. Rebecca will be fine. She's just wandered a bit too far away. We will find her. Kenneth let's gather up some sticks and make a pile here to mark where we were. We will lay out a few leading out to the field so we can find our way back to this spot. Charles, can you help?" I asked as I set him down.

"Yes, Mama," he said, still a bit tearfully.

We quickly set to the task. Thankfully it was still morning, and we would have light for some hours to come, but it would be very cold in the forest come nightfall. We must find her before then. As soon as we marked our spot, we hurried back to the house. I used the rifle to signal for help, two shots quickly together and then one a few minutes later. This was the signal we had always used in our community, and it has always rallied us to help each other in times of need. I think the last time anyone used this was Thomas Brownson when their farm was on fire.

"Kenneth, wait at the road so that the neighbors will know it is us. I will join you soon but tell anyone who comes that Rebecca is missing in the forest," I said. "Charles, would you like to go visit with Miss Brooke?"

"Yes, Mama," he said excitedly.

I ran as quickly as Charles could go to Charlotte's house, encountering Fuller already on his way to our house.

"Mrs. Wagner, was it you that signaled?"

"Yes, Fuller. It is Rebecca. She wandered away from us while we were in the forest looking for our Christmas tree. I was hoping Brooke could watch Charles while we search," I said nearly out of breath.

"Of course. I will rejoin you in a moment."

Without another word, he scooped Charles into his arms and hurried with him into the house while I returned to the road to wait with Kenneth. I could see a wagon coming in the distance with several people and a man on horseback. Soon all the men from the neighborhood were assembled in front of our house and I told everyone what had happened.

"The women and older children can help too," said Thomas.

"Jeremiah, take my horse and ride to each house and tell the women who are able that they should come with the older children," said David.

Fuller, with Charlotte right behind, joined the group and soon there were nearly twenty of us. Thomas quickly took charge and arranged the searchers into groups so that each would have a man with a rifled musket or breech loader in case anyone should encounter a small black bear or wolf. Once all was arranged, we headed off to the spot where we had last been.

"Millie, it was very smart of you to mark this place so that we could find it again," said Thomas as we arrived at the spot.

"What color is her coat?" asked Fuller.

"Brown, her coat is brown," I replied, realizing that would

allow her to blend in rather than stand out which made my heart sink.

"We will find her," said Charlotte as she reached over and squeezed my hand.

The groups set out under Thomas's direction, instructed to return to the marked spot if a shot was fired. In moments, cries of "Rebecca" echoed through the trees again. I walked with Mr. Brown. Kenneth had gone with Mr. Wilson. Charlotte and Fuller went together. Group after group of neighbors spread out into the dense forest, soon losing sight of each other. Mr. Brown and I did not speak but called out for Rebecca every few minutes, stopping to listen quietly for any noise or response after each call.

"Thank you, Mr. Brown, for helping," I said finally as we walked along.

"Lewis, ma'am, please call me Lewis," he replied, tipping his hat to me as we continued walking.

"Thank you truly, Lewis. Do you have children?" I asked.

"I do. A son, Arthur, but he is only three ma'am."

I smiled. Lewis looked to be about thirty. He was a handsome man with a long beard and a slight build. He did not seem familiar to me, and I wondered where he lived.

"We live in Kimball, some six miles or so from here. My wife, Candace, Arthur and I are here visiting my friend, David

Morgan. We grew up near each other in New York."

"Of course, there are many of us here from New York, as Matthew and I are," I replied.

"David told me of your plight. I am sorry, truly. I will pray for your husband's safe return," he said.

"Thank you," I replied before we turned our attention back to the task at hand, calling out for Rebecca.

The sun had moved on, no longer directly overhead, and my hands and feet were numb from the cold. I could only imagine how Rebecca must be feeling. I sat down on a fallen log to rub my feet when I heard a booming sound in the distance.

"Lewis, was that a shot?"

"Yes, ma'am I believe it is," he said as he helped me up from the log and we quickly headed back to the meeting place. It seemed to take an eternity to get back to the clearing where we had started. When we reached it, several other groups were already there, but I did not see Rebecca.

"They have taken her up to the house Mrs. Wagner," said Jeremiah gesturing in that direction, "We will wait here till everyone returns."

I ran past him yelling my thanks as I reached the edge of the field. My legs felt like I was running through mud even though the ground was hard and cold. Each step was a new agony as my legs burned from the effort, feeling both cold and hot at the same time. By the time I reached the back door I barely had the strength to open it and tumble inside.

"My goodness Millicent, here sit down," said Charlotte as she grabbed me and kept me from falling to the floor.

"Rebecca," I wheezed out trying to catch my breath.

"Cold and tired but otherwise unharmed. I sent for the doctor though just to be sure, but she's warm in bed now and sleeping," she replied.

"I can't afford the doctor," I said looking at her in dismay.

"I'll take care of it, no need to worry," said Charlotte as she set down a cup of tea in front of me.

"My dear friend, I do not know how we would survive were it not for you," I said holding the warm cup in both my hands and feeling the thawing of my fingers.

"It is as friends do for each other if they can," she said matter-of-factly.

As soon as I could stand, I went back outside and thanked each group in turn as they passed the house on their way to their carriages and horses on the road.

Kenneth and Mr. Wilson had found her quite a distance from where we had last seen her. She had been following an unusual bird. She told them she wanted to see where it lived and how it stayed warm when it was so cold. She seemed neither frightened nor worried, haplessly unaware of the danger she was in and the fuss she had caused. Kenneth was sound asleep as well, exhausted from the day's efforts, as was I. Brooke brought Charles back after feeding him a small supper. He and I both climbed into my bed together and slept.

Rebecca had no explanation for her behavior other than the fact that she was watching the bird and got distracted. She seemed no worse for the wear, although the doctor suggested that she needed to have more supervision to ensure she did not do anything to hurt herself or someone else. I do my very best to keep an eye on her, and I do not leave her alone with Charles. Kenneth, I am assuming, could defend himself if she tried to do something to him as she had to Cordelia. She is not an evil child. She just seems to be unable to control herself in some situations and is oblivious to how her actions might impact others. Since Matthew has been gone, it does seem that she is worse, having more angry outbursts and being more difficult. She is just the opposite of Kenneth who could not be more helpful and cooperative.

Over the next two weeks, we decorated our tree with candied fruit and popcorn balls. We hung stockings on the fireplace in the parlor for Father Christmas. It seemed strange to hang just the three stockings this year and it made me feel

Cordelia's loss more profoundly, as if that were even possible. I wondered what kind of Christmas Mariah was having and if she was delivered yet of her child. A grandmother… I wondered if I shall ever even meet him or her.

December 1862

Dearest Millicent,

I am grateful for the chance to write you to say that I am holding up as well as I can under the circumstances. No need to go into the details of my capture except to say in some way I am grateful, given the number of my fellow soldiers who fell that day. The sergeant in charge of the stockade I am kept in is unkind, but not cruel, as I have seen some of the others be. We have a bit of rice and bread, water, and occasional vegetables but seldom any meat. There is talk every day of prisoner exchanges, and so I am hopeful that I may be released soon. We can hear the fighting going on in the distance and it pains me to know the Union army is so close to me. I am forced every few days to work on shoeing horses for the enemy and it pains me to do this knowing I am enabling them to ride out and kill more of us, but I was rather badly beaten the first time I refused. I will not do so again. My goal now is to survive this so that I may come home to you and the children. Know that my love for you never wavers, and I hope to hold you soon.

Your loving husband,

Matthew

Christmas is a quiet affair with just one small wooden truck for Charles, a pocketknife for Kenneth (which he needed more than wanted), and two hair ribbons for Rebecca. I was also given some oranges and sweets by Charlotte which made the day a bit more festive. It was hard to think of what Matthew might be enduring today and every day. Yesterday I finally told the children that their father had been captured. Kenneth took the news with great difficulty, and it seemed to upset him more than I had imagined it would. Perhaps he felt some pride knowing his father was fighting and it justified his absence, but now he was merely gone, wasting away in a prison camp. Rebecca and Charles seemed to pay it no mind.

I decided not to tell Matthew about Cordelia, feeling he was already so burdened that he did not need to carry this as well. There is nothing he can do or could have done that would have changed the outcome. Only God controls such things. Will the enemy give him letters if I were to send them? I sincerely doubt it. Southerners are dying in our prison camps too. Of that, I have no doubt. This war does not discriminate when it comes to inflicting pain and suffering. There is much to go around.

As he had said that he would, President Lincoln enacted the Emancipation Proclamation declaring all enslaved people in rebel states to be free as well as authorizing the enlistment of black troops. Southerners by all accounts were enraged by this action, but it is clear that Lincoln means to not just restore the Union but to make it better, into a country without slavery.

The winter has been bitterly cold, although not much snow has fallen. Our trips out to the barn are frigid indeed. Kenneth really needs a new coat, as the one he is wearing is much too small. Rebecca needs new shoes, although she was able to wear a pair that had belonged to Cordelia as well as a few of her other clothes. My own coat has been mended and patched but it will have to do for now as there is simply no money to purchase a new one. We will have to sell Moon's foal in the spring in the yearling sale and I'm hopeful that it will generate enough money for us to make it through until the garden begins to produce again.

The paper has announced the birth of a baby, a boy to be named William Addison Parker after his grandfather. Mariah is now a mother, and I am a grandmother. I can't help but wonder if Matthew will ever know he is a grandfather. Truly, I thought he would be released by now. There is talk in the paper every week of prisoner exchanges and yet the Army has no new information to offer even though it has been nearly five months. Brooke is kind enough to check with them every time she is in town, waiting patiently for her chance to inquire, as the lines of women waiting grow longer every week. With spring also comes lines of men, as those between the ages of eighteen and thirty-five are now being conscripted for service. They wait their turn to be listed on the roster and told where to report and when. These past months there were many times I had wished that Kenneth were older but today, I am grateful he is only fourteen.

Once again, I am indebted to Fuller, and Charlotte, for his help with the tilling as we work to prepare the land so that we can plant the hay and garden. It has been a year and a half now since we planted the full field and weeds and grasses are beginning to take over. Kenneth is a greater help now as he continues to grow in stature and strength. Perhaps next year he could manage the plow on his own. Next year? How could I even fathom that Matthew would not be home with us for another year? Surely, he will be rescued or released before then. I never think that he may die in captivity. It would break my heart to think of him dying in that way, such a futile and terrible waste of a life… of his life.

"Children, we are going into town tomorrow, first thing in the morning," I said at breakfast.

"What for?" said Kenneth as he slurped his coffee heavy with milk.

"We are going to sell the foal and get a few things we

need, and if the price is good enough, a new coat for you, shoes for your sister, and long pants for Charles," I said almost defiantly as if I were daring the world to interfere with my plans. This foal needs to fetch a good price if we are to get the things we need. Otherwise, I will have to consider some other means of generating money, although how escapes my mind at this moment. I suppose I could see if one of the neighbors would be interested in purchasing a few acres of the farm, but I do not know how Matthew might react to that decision. He was always wanting more land, not less, and so I'm afraid that decision might be met with a great deal of consternation on his part.

Kenneth and Rebecca managed to hook up the wagon to Moon without any help from me which is the first time that has occurred. It would be a slower journey with just one horse, but the wagon would not be heavily loaded so it should be manageable for her. The foal would be tied to the back, and she should be able to keep up easily at the wagon's slower pace.

"Do we have to sell the pony? I love her," whined Charles as he climbed into the wagon.

"Yes, my precious, I am afraid we do," I replied as I took the reins, Kenneth next to me and Rebecca in the back with her brother.

"Tck, tck," I clicked to Moon and away she went with no further prodding from me.

The road was just barely damp, but not so much that it would slow the wagon. There were very few others on the road, save a horse and rider from time to time.

"Kenneth, would you like to drive?" I asked.

He beamed at me. "Yes, I would very much!"

"All right then. Take the reins son, and remember you control the wagon. The wagon does not control you. Remember the safety of all of us depends on your attention and skill."

He did wonderfully, anticipating obstacles and large ruts. I could not have been prouder of him. I know Matthew had let him drive around the farm some but to be on the road into town was a whole new experience and it was a day I was sure he would remember for some time. When we arrived at the horse auction I took over, guiding the wagon into an open space.

"Kenneth, stay here with the wagon and keep an eye on Rebecca and Charles," I said as I untied the foal and led her into the barn, stopping just a moment for Moon to nuzzle her one last time.

The auction was well underway when I arrived and there were several women there doing just as I was, finding a way to generate income in the absence of a man in the house. The foal was a beautiful animal, and several came over to admire her so I was optimistic that when her turn came, she would bring a good price. The bidding started at eighty dollars and ninety was quickly reached, then one hundred. Then, one hundred ten. My heart was pounding. Things were going well, and I knew it would go higher with so many horses being taken for the cavalry. Farms needed horses for wagons and carriages.

"One twenty," a man called out from the back, bidding against the man near the railing in the bright red jacket.

"One thirty," he replied without hesitation.

"One forty," the voice in the back called out. I could not see him from where I stood.

"One sixty," said the man in the red jacket, clearly frustrated that he was being bid against.

"Two hundred," was the reply and I could not help but gasp.

The man in the red jacket looked back at the filly as the auctioneer held up his gavel, but it was clear he would go no higher.

"Sold for two hundred dollars to Mr. John Parker," he said as he banged the gavel down onto the podium.

While the crowd applauded, I looked around confused. I

did not see him in the barn, but it was crowded. Did he know he was buying a horse from me? Did he pay more than the foal was worth as a kind of… charity? My stomach churned at the thought, but there was nothing to be done now. I waited behind another man at the auctioneer's table for payment.

"What is this?" the man in front of me demanded as the auctioneer's assistant handed him a stack of green paper.

"That, sir, is your money. Greenbacks," said the assistant.

"I don't want this trash. I want coins! Gold and silver. This is not money," he shouted his voice rising over the calls of the auctioneer.

"Sir, please lower your voice," cried out the auctioneer before resuming the bidding.

"This is the only form of money we have. You can take this, or you take your horses. Which is it going to be?"

The man looked at the papers in his hand and cursed at the man behind the desk before turning and taking his leave.

"What is this greenback?" I asked when it was my turn.

"Government-issued paper money ma'am. It's as good as coins and backed by these United States," he said as he counted out one hundred and ninety-eight dollars, which was my proceeds minus the auctioneer's fee.

"You are sure?" I asked hesitantly.

"Yes, I am sure this is the only money we have used for the last month or so and everyone is getting on just fine. They will take it at the bank or Cooks or anywhere in town you may want to use it. Now, some people might not want it, but before long it will be all there is."

"Thank you," I said as folded the papers and tucked them inside my dress, keeping it safe against my chest. This was even more money than I had gotten for the bull, and it would allow us to manage for some time.

As I left the barn I glanced around to see if John Parker could be located but I never saw him. We had quite a shopping spree at Cooks, getting everything we needed. As the young man had said, the paper money worked just fine.

Chapter Eight - *That Which is Necessary*

Our trip to Port Huron yesterday was fruitful. I was very happy with the result of the sale and what we were able to purchase with the proceeds. The children were happy too and enjoyed a couple of hard candies on the ride home, which was a real treat for them. I even felt a bit of happiness this morning while milking the cows and enjoying the warm air. I was surprised to see the Deputy Constable and Mr. Cook walking up the path to the house so early in the morning.

"Good morning, Mr. Cook, Constable," I said as I wiped my hands on my apron.

"Good morning to you Mrs. Wagner," said the Constable.

"Is Kenneth here?" asked Mr. Cook.

"Of course, he's in the house. What is this about?" I asked, starting to feel a bit of concern.

"When you were in the store yesterday, Kenneth took a bracelet from a tray that my wife had on the counter to show Mrs. Sherman," said Mr. Cook.

I was stunned. We had raised all of our children with respect for others and their property. Stealing is something they certainly know is forbidden by both God and man. And truly, what reason would he have?

"Surely you must be mistaken. I cannot believe my son would do such a thing. Why do you believe it is Kenneth?"

"I spoke with several people who had been in the store during the same time you and your son were there. He was identified as the boy who had been standing next to the counter around the time as the bracelet went missing," replied the Constable.

"Could we speak with Kenneth, ma'am?" added Mr. Cook.

"Certainly, come into the house, please. I'm sure we can clear this up quickly," I replied.

I stood in the doorway of the parlor as the Constable and Mr. Cook spoke with Kenneth. As I had anticipated, he denied taking the bracelet and he seemed calm and unafraid, unlike someone who had something to hide. Finally, the men left, seemingly satisfied that they were mistaken, and that Kenneth was not the person they were looking for. I spoke to him about it that evening, and he denied that he had anything to do with the missing bracelet. I believed him, and it was quickly forgotten.

The paper brought news of the Battle of Chancellorsville in Virginia. General Hooker, leading the Union forces, had a plan to attack General Lee but it was a failure once again. The

Confederates had suffered very high losses. Perhaps of most significance was the mortal wounding of General "Stonewall" Jackson who reports say died a few days later. That devil Jefferson Davis, the so-called President of the Confederated States, is so incensed by the Emancipation Proclamation he has responded with the Retaliatory Act. It says that the Confederacy sees the inclusion of black troops in the war to be inciting a slave rebellion and that white officers of black troops who are captured are to be executed. Furthermore, any black troops captured are to be sent to the Southern states where they could be executed or enslaved once more.

The barbarity of this war cannot be overstated. The level of inhumanity we have seen shakes me to the core. The few men who have returned to the area, having been wounded in the fighting, speak of the terrible toll this war is taking. The fields are covered with the blood and human remains of the men, on both sides, who are dying by the droves in defense of an idea. The simple concept of men, all men, being entitled to live a life where they are in control of their labor and happiness. It seems so simple, really. It is hard to reconcile that this concept has brought to us all this pain, suffering, and death.

May 1863

Dear Mrs. Wagner,

We are writing to inform you that your husband, Sargent Matthew Wagner of the Michigan 6th Calvary Company C, has been moved from the Confederate prison camp known as Belle Isle to an unknown prison in the South.

I am sorry that my letter does not bring you better news but know the United States Army and government are doing their utmost to recover all prisoners of war and bring this conflict to a conclusion. There is no further status report as to his condition. You may communicate with your nearest Army office for additional reports as they become available.

Yours respectfully,

Lieutenant Arthur Wilson

Michigan Calvary Regiment Assistant Commander

I sat on the back porch reading the letter and looking out on the farm, which seemed so bucolic in this moment. The breeze was light. The air smelled of summer and possibilities, a future that I could not see. What would my future be without Matthew? I had not allowed myself to think of it, to consider that he might not return to me… but it seems as though God may have other plans. Truly, how long can he survive what by all accounts are the most horrendous of circumstances? Perhaps he is being more beneficially treated because of his blacksmithing skills, but still, these places are fraught with dysentery and disease and even Matthew's constitution can only bear that for so long.

This land should be worked. It should provide crops to feed the hungry and work for men who need it. If I sold the farm and he did return, we could always use the money to buy another farm nearby and start again I suppose. But what would I do? Where would I go? I had no idea. We had talked about my returning to New York to live near our families there, but that would mean leaving the graves of my children and of course Mariah and the baby. Although I did not see them, it warmed my heart to know they were nearby. When we talked of this, Mariah was still with me, and Cordelia was still alive. Would he feel any differently today? I could try to write him, but I've not heard from him directly for many months now, and it is clear this is a decision I must make on my own.

To that end, I sent one letter to Bessie and another to Matthew's brother, Shubal, to see what their thoughts are on the matter. Until then, the work of the farm must continue as best we can and the three of us work tirelessly. Charles is doing very well in school and every night Kenneth helps him with his reading and math. These two have a close bond, as brothers should, and Kenneth is very patient with him. Rebecca has no tolerance for schoolwork and now it seems she can barely read, having forgotten most of what she learned.

"See what I did, Mama?" says Charles proudly showing me the letters in his primer that are written in very neat cursive.

"That is very good Charles! You should be very proud of yourself," I said, smiling at him as I put away the last of the supper dishes.

"It's not very good at all," quipped Rebecca.

"Rebecca, why would you say such a thing? It's very good. Apologize to your brother at once," I said sternly.

"No," she snapped at me before lunging at Charles and pushing him and his chair backward, crashing them both to the floor with a loud thud. Charles cried out in pain and as I picked him up, I could see a bit of blood on the floor.

"You are hateful!" screamed Kenneth as he slapped Rebecca across the face. Her cheek instantly turned a deep crimson red before he spun around to help Charles up from the floor.

"Enough!" I screamed in a voice I didn't even recognize.

Rebecca sat down at the kitchen table like nothing had

even happened while Kenneth and I tried to calm Charles and clean up the mess. The blood was from a small cut on the back of his head, and I was able to clean it up easily, but it could have been much worse. That night, after Charles and Rebecca had gone to bed, Kenneth knocked on my bedroom door.

"Mama, can I talk to you?"

"Of course. Come in," I said as I gestured toward the empty chair.

"Mama, you have to do something about Rebecca," he said with a serious tone.

"Kenneth, I know what happened tonight was very unfortunate, and you shouldn't have hit her. You know she cannot always control herself. She didn't mean to hurt Charles," I replied.

"But she did hurt him, and she does these things all the time. Sometimes, you don't know that she is hitting us. She even stabbed me with a pencil," he said lifting his shirt to show me a small scar on his stomach.

"When did that happen? You should have told me," I chastised.

"Why? What good would it do? You never do anything about what she does. A few months ago, she was playing with matches in the barn, she could have burned the whole thing down," he said nearly in tears.

"Oh, my son, I had no idea. You should have told me," I said, nearly in tears myself as I gathered him into my arms and hugged him to me tightly.

"Please, Mama, before something really bad happens. Please do something with her," he said at last.

"I will see what can be done, I promise. But if anything else happens you must tell me at once. No secrets. Do you understand?"

He nodded and left the room, closing the door behind him. I stared into the flames licking the log in the fireplace. In my heart, I knew that Rebecca had been getting worse, but I could not face it. How can I possibly choose between my children? Is it reasonable to keep Rebecca here? If I do, can I keep us all safe? If she had burned down the barn and killed the livestock, I don't know what we would have done. What if the fire had spread to the house? I had no idea it was this bad… but I also have no plan for what to do. It was becoming quite clear that a failure to act on my part could have serious consequences. So far, her attacks have resulted in minor wounds, but they all could have been much more serious. Tomorrow I will speak to Charlotte. Maybe she could offer some advice for a way forward.

I loved sitting in this parlor. The room was warm and

inviting and the view of the garden was spectacular. The sofa was plush, both firm and soft at the same time and I always felt so peaceful sitting here, as if my problems were far away where they could not reach me.

"Millicent, I can see something is on your mind. What it is dear?" said Charlotte as soon as Brooke had left the room.

"Rebecca," I replied taking a sip of my tea. It was hot and fragrant and warmed me through and through.

"Ah, I see," she replied setting down her cup. "Has something happened?"

"Yes, and things have been happening of which I was not aware. Dangerous things that could have had a devastating effect on our family. She pushed Charles over in a chair a few days ago, and afterward, Kenneth came to me and told me about the other things she had done that were not in my sight. He also begged me to do something with her before something very bad happened," I said reluctantly.

"It is a most difficult situation to be sure. I can understand why Kenneth has come to you. I did much the same with my own mother about Deborah," she said as she looked out the window as if seeing another day or another time, somewhere in the past.

"My sister was a good child when she was young. She was sweet and caring, but the older she got the more she changed.

The angry outbursts and the hitting and spitting at people became more common. It was as if she had been possessed by something, and it changed who she was. When I was fourteen, she stabbed me with a kitchen knife, and it was not the first time she had stabbed someone. She was never a good student, but by the time she reached twenty, she was unable to read or do even basic chores around the house, having forgotten how. But it was a situation with our housekeeper, Mrs. Twillen, that changed everything."

"I am sorry, Charlotte. You don't have to tell me more if you are uncomfortable," I said at last, as she continued to gaze out the window.

"No, I think you need to know Millicent, for your own sake and the sake of your children. Deborah pushed Mrs. Twillen down the stairs during a fit of anger and she died. After that, Mother kept her in her room. She was only allowed outside for occasional walks. She was never part of the family again. She did not even attend my parents' funerals as she is too untrustworthy. After Mother died, Leo and I moved her, as I had told you before, to a place where they could care for her. I could not bear having her locked up in my own home," she said as her eyes returned to mine, and I could see the profound sadness in them.

"Oh, Charlotte, I am so very sorry for your pain."

"You need to think carefully, Millicent, about your situation. It could very well be that Rebecca causes the death of someone in your household. Not that she would mean to, but as you can see, she really can't help herself," she replied.

I leaned back into the sofa, wishing it could just swallow me up so I could disappear and not have to think about this situation. I had never felt Matthew's absence more than I did at this very moment. My mind swirled with so many thoughts I was not able to put them in any kind of order. Charlotte looked at me carefully.

"I have a way forward for you Millie, but it will not be an easy path. You will need to be strong to make this kind of decision," she said softly.

Charlotte never called me Millie. It sounded odd coming from her. I don't know why out of all the things she had said to me this morning, that would be the one that stuck out in my mind, but it was.

"I'm listening," I replied.

"I could speak to the Director at the Daughters of Charity and see if they would allow Rebecca to come and share a room with Deborah. They are very well trained there, and they would take good care of Rebecca. Sharing a room would keep the cost more manageable, and I would be happy to make up the additional expense if that were something you would consider."

My heart sank. Send my daughter to a mental institution? She's not crazy, is she? Difficult, unpredictable, unaware, dangerous, yes. But what makes someone crazy, really? I do not even know for certain. Did Rebecca fall into that category? What was becoming crystal clear was that she could not be trusted either alone or with others. I could not watch her every minute of every day. I needed someone who could.

"That is very generous of you Charlotte, but wouldn't you be worried that Rebecca might do something to hurt Deborah?"

"That is true, but Deborah could just as easily be the one to hurt Rebecca. They do not allow patients to have items that could be used as weapons, and they sleep with their doors open so that they can be monitored even at night. It is a risk for both of us to be sure, but one I am willing to entertain if you are?"

My tears began to flow. Charlotte joined me on the sofa, putting her arms around me and holding me while I sobbed, harder than I had for some time. When my tears finally ended, I looked at Charlotte and she used her handkerchief to wipe my face.

"I will send a letter today," she said as she studied my

face.

I nodded my agreement, unable to even speak. This would be best. Rebecca could be taken care of, Kenneth and Charles would be safe, and I could visit her from time to time. She might even be happy there. True to her word, Charlotte wrote to the Director and it was arranged. A nurse would come by train to collect Rebecca at the station in Port Huron and take her back to Detroit in just a few days. Kenneth was very relieved and even Charles seemed to understand that this was for the best.

Rebecca reacted in a most positive way, excited about going on an adventure and she seemed unconcerned by the idea that her family wouldn't be going with her. Would she even miss us? I wasn't sure if she was capable of that. She never said I love you, or any real expression of fondness, honestly. I realized now that she never really had. As I packed up her few possessions, I found a small doll that had belonged to Cordelia. She had misplaced it some time ago and she had been inconsolable at its loss. It appears now that Rebecca had taken it and hidden it away all this time. I also found the hair clip I had given Mariah for her sixteenth birthday, and the toy wooden train we had given Charles. She had been taking and hiding things belonging to her siblings for some time, it appears.

I left the doll and hairclip with her things, but I set Charles' train aside. I would give it back to him after she left. Fuller arrived with the carriage at the appointed hour and Rebecca said her goodbyes to her brothers. No embraces were exchanged, and Kenneth set off to take Charles to school as we headed in the other direction. The ride passed quickly, too quickly, and Rebecca was quiet but observant as she watched all the trees and birds as we went down the road. She had always liked to watch birds, sometimes obsessively, as we had all learned last winter when she wandered into the woods and got lost.

The train station was busy with soldiers departing for their assignments and there were many women and children there saying their goodbyes. We waited together on the edge of the platform, anticipating the train's arrival.

"I will write to you Rebecca, and you can write to me as well. One of the nurses will help you," I said as I heard the train approaching.

"Yes, Mama," she said without any intonation.

"You need to be a good girl, and I am sure you will make new friends and have a grand time in your new home," I said as I held back the tears.

"Yes, Mama," she said again.

When the train reached the station, several soldiers got

off. Most were wounded and required assistance from Army medical staff who were waiting on the platform. I saw a woman in a white dress and hat, very much like that worn by Mrs. O'Connell. She had on a small red scarf, which was our signal that this was the nurse from the charity.

"Hello," I said waving to get her attention.

"Mrs. Wagner?" she asked as she approached us.

"Yes, and this is Rebecca," I replied.

"Hello, Rebecca, I am Miss Davison. You are going to come with me to your new house, yes?" she asked.

"Yes ma'am," she replied.

"Mrs. Wagner, I promise you that we will take very good care of Rebecca and please do come and visit whenever you can. Deborah is looking forward to having a new friend and I'm confident the girls will get on quite well," she said smiling.

She seemed like such a pleasant person, and it made me feel better about turning Rebecca over to her. It was just a minute later that the train blew its whistle, alerting passengers that it would be starting its return trip to Detroit shortly.

"We should board, Rebecca," said Miss Davison as she took her by the hand.

"I love you, Rebecca. I will come visit you soon," I said as I held her tightly, kissing her on the cheek.

"Bye, Mama," she said as she followed the nurse onto the

train.

I could see Rebecca sitting next to the window expressionless, just staring out the window, but not truly seeing. I waved to her, but she did not respond. The train whistle blew again, and I stepped back as the train belched steam and the pistons pumped, propelling the train forward. In just a few moments it was well on its way down the tracks.

As I boarded the carriage for the ride back to the house, I was hopeful that I had made the right decision, and that this was what was best for us all. I hoped she would be happy. Now there is one less person to help around the house and garden, such as she offered, and I just don't see how Kenneth and I can manage on our own. We will have to sell the farm.

Chapter Nine - *The Season of Change*

Gettysburg. It was a name I had not heard before, but now it is on everyone's lips and first and foremost in every newspaper. *A massive victory for the Union and a crushing blow to the Confederates,* the papers all said. But at what cost? Twenty-three thousand losses on the Union side and nearly thirty thousand of Lee's men, which is almost a third of his army. The line of wagons carrying the wounded back to the South stretched for seventeen miles. It was clear now that General Lee would no longer try to move farther into the North but would focus more on maintaining the states they already held. But what has changed? Nothing, really. The war still raged on throughout the summer, although the Union continued to make inroads in the South. The war that people said would be over in two weeks is now over two years and counting.

Kenneth and I worked hard to keep up the farm. I had not told him yet that we would need to sell. I thought waiting until fall would be best. Once we had done all we could to sustain ourselves for the winter, I would try to sell the farm and we would move to town. We would save as much as we could from the sale so that when Matthew returns, we could buy another farm if that is what he wishes to do. We celebrated Charles' seventh birthday, but just the three of us seemed so odd. We have gone from being a family of seven to a table that holds more chairs than people. I receive an update from the charity every other month and Rebecca seems to have settled in there with no issues. Charlotte says that come spring, the two of us will go and visit, which I am very much looking forward to.

Bessie and Shubal both responded to my letters and welcomed us to return there, but with Rebecca now in Detroit, I am reluctant to move so far away that I cannot visit her. If anything, I would like to be closer to her so that I can visit more often. Moving to Port Huron will accomplish that. Then I can go by boat or train to the city to see her more easily.

"Mama, when is Papa coming home?" asked Charles unexpectedly as we sat down to supper.

"I wish I knew my dear, but it is in God's hands. Only he knows when your father will return," I replied.

"I don't think he's coming home," mumbled Kenneth.

"Why would you say such a thing?"

"I went to see Mr. Fuller to ask him to help me with fixing an ax I had broken, and he told me all about the prison camps. They are horrid places he said, where the men kept there have little food or water and there is rampant sickness and disease. He called it hell on earth," said Kenneth looking at me as if defying me to say something to the contrary.

"That is true, what he said. Prison camps are awful, awful places and yes… many men die there. But your father is a very strong man, and he wants to come home very badly. We must have hope that he will come back to us," I replied with more confidence than I really felt.

"I think if father were coming back, he would have come by now," said Kenneth.

"What will happen if Papa doesn't come home?" said Charles looking up at me with sadness in his eyes.

"We will have to sell the farm. Won't we, Mama?" said Kenneth.

I very much did not want to have this conversation now, but it seemed that it could not wait.

"Yes, if your father does not return by the end of the summer, I will sell the farm and we will move to Port Huron where we can find a small house. Charles, you can go to school there, and Kenneth you can find work perhaps at the stable where your father did his shoeing," I said trying to keep my voice pleasant and optimistic.

Kenneth pushed back his chair from the table so quickly

that it fell over with a thud as he ran out the back door.

"Kenneth," I called after him, but he ran off without looking back.

I went to the window and saw him running into the barn.

"Mama why is Kenneth mad?" asked Charles.

"Oh, darling boy he's not mad. He's just upset at the idea of having to leave the farm. He loves it here. I do too, but sometimes things must change even though we don't want them to."

It was time I spoke to someone in the Army myself so that I could determine what the right course of action might be. Was my husband going to come home or not? Surely someone could tell me something as anything was better than just not knowing. After we dropped Charles at school, Kenneth and I headed into town. Mrs. Smith, the teacher, would take Charles home with her where we could collect him later if we did not return before school adjourned. Kenneth said little as we rode together but he did drive the wagon the entire way and did a fine job. As we tied up in front of the courthouse next door to the Army office, I finally broke the silence.

"Kenneth, I am going to give you thirty cents you can spend at Cooks on whatever you would like. I have lunch for you here in this bag which I'll leave in the wagon. You can wait in the wagon or go to the park by the river, but please do not get too close to the water's edge. Or if you like, you can come with me to the Army office."

"I will go to the park," he said quietly.

"That is fine son. If you are not at the wagon when I return, I will come and look for you there," I said before I leaned over to kiss him on the cheek, but he pulled away.

I could see that he was still very upset, but I hope he will come to understand that he and I cannot possibly manage the farm alone and that Charles is several years away from being able to contribute any meaningful help. The line at the Army office was long, and several women were wiping away tears as they waited quietly. No one talked unless it was to someone who was waiting with them, and the time passed slowly. My feet began to ache, and I could feel beads of sweat running down my back. Thankfully a young soldier was going up and down the line with a bucket and cup offering water to us, which was most appreciated.

Finally, it was my turn to speak to the man who sat at one of the three desks in the room I was shown to. The chair in front of his desk was most appreciated.

"How may I help you ma'am?" asked Second Lieutenant A. Jones as he looked up from the papers in front of him.

"My husband, Sargent Matthew Wagner, Michigan 6th

Cavalry, Company C was taken prisoner at the battle of Antietam. He was taken to Belle Isle prison, but I was told a few months ago that he had been moved to somewhere in the South. Can you tell me anything more about where he might be and if he is well?"

"I am sorry for your plight Mrs. Wagner, but our information is somewhat limited. Give me one moment please," he said as he went into another room where I could see him opening a large filing cabinet and thumbing through some papers. He returned in a few minutes with a paper in hand. I could see it had Matthew's name at the top, but I could read nothing below it.

"Your husband was alive as of a month ago. This is based on a report received from a soldier from his company who managed to escape from the place where he and your husband were being held, along with other soldiers. The name of that encampment is unknown. We believe it was only a temporary way station as the Confederates continue to move prisoners to avoid their liberation as Union forces push them farther south."

"Well, that is some good news," I replied.

"It is ma'am. I am afraid I know nothing about your husband's health as nothing was reported to us," he added.

"Do you have any idea if there will be any further

prisoner exchanges?" I asked hopefully.

"No ma'am, I do not believe so. General Grant is not in favor even though Johnny Reb would like us to. They need their men back because there are many more of us than them, but the General says he's not releasing these men so they can go back to the battlefield and kill more Union soldiers."

"I would share that concern, but he may be sacrificing the lives of those men who are in their prisons. Namely my husband," I said earnestly.

"He is aware of that Mrs. Wagner, truly he is. But he believes that by reducing the number of Rebs on the battlefield, we will bring this conflict to an end sooner, freeing your husband and all the others," he said sincerely.

"If he survives that long…"

"I am sorry ma'am. You have my sincere hope and prayer that it will be soon. Is there anything else I can do for you?"

I looked over my shoulder at the still-long line of women waiting outside, and I knew my time was up. Many others were waiting to talk to Lieutenant Jones. Someone else who was desperate to sit in this chair, desperate to find out what was happening to their loved one, desperate to get them home.

Kenneth was waiting at the wagon and once again we

made the trip back to the farm without speaking. I could only hope he would forgive me and come to understand that we have no choice. I hope we can find a place where we can keep a few of the animals, the ewe lamb Charles is so fond of, one of the cows, the chickens, and of course Moon. Perhaps that would make it more palatable for him, and honestly for all of us.

The garden has been harvested and the hay is stacked in the barn. Once again, the fields are bare and the larder full. It will be a long winter. Kenneth is nearly six years older than Charles and he is no longer interested in playing the games that Charles likes. It will be difficult to keep them both busy, but I am hoping that one of them will take an interest in helping me with the baking and mending which at this point all falls to me. Kenneth has taken over all the milking, mucking of stalls, feeding the cows, and caring for Moon. Charles collects the eggs and throws out the feed for the chickens, so there is little for me to do outside at least.

Over the last few days, I've gone from neighbor to neighbor to let them know that I am interested in selling the farm. David thought perhaps his friend Lewis Brown might like to buy it. He was the man who had walked with me when Rebecca was lost. He is a very nice man with a young and growing family. That would be a good arrangement. We worked out the details over the space of just a few days and once again Fuller was there to help me. Charlotte was very unhappy at the prospect of us moving to town.

"Millicent, I wish you would let me help you so that you and the children could stay here on the farm," she said as she sat at my kitchen table.

"Charlotte, you have done so much for us already. Too much, truth be known. I can never repay your kindness or the money I owe you. But I believe it is time to make a change and put us into a situation that we can manage on our own."

"You know you are very welcome to stay with us until Matthew… until you understand whether or not Matthew is coming home," she said with the directness I have come to expect from her.

"I know the tide of the war seems to be changing. Just last week the Union broke up the Rebel siege in Chattanooga which sent General Bragg scurrying like a rat back into Georgia. But still, no word on my husband, and so I feel like I cannot wait any longer," I said with an air of resignation.

"I understand, and I hope we can see each other whenever I am in town. Know this, my dear friend, if there is anything that I can do to help you and the children, you need only ask. And of course, we will go to visit Deborah and Rebecca in the spring," she said. As she looked at me her eyes began to shine with the glint of a tear.

"You have been a most wonderful friend to me and my family. I hope sincerely that we can continue this relationship, if maybe not quite so easily or often," I said as I rose and embraced her.

Dear Millicent,

This may well be my last letter to you. We are being moved again and I doubt letters will be possible as we head farther south. I am well mostly; having lost so much weight you may not even recognize me when I come home. Surely you are still sending letters to me but sadly I no longer get them. I don't have much faith that this will reach you, but I will try. Should I speak what is in my heart, I would say that I am sorry to have left you and the children in this situation… but know that I trust you fully to make the decisions you must. If you decide to go back to New York, I will find you there, so do not worry. For the first time in these many months, I am not sure that I will make it back to you. Know that the great treasure of my life has been you and the children and if I do not survive this, I will go to God safe in the knowledge that I have been loved and that my love for you will live on, always.

Matthew

While my heart feels heavy, I take comfort in knowing that deciding to sell the farm is an act that Matthew would not only understand but would bless. We have been very fortunate to find a small house at the end of Elmwood Street with a barn on the edge of town. I bought it with some of the money from the farm. We will have room for two cows, Moon, and of course, the lamb which is now a fully grown ewe. There is even a chicken coop, but it needs a bit of repair before we can move the chickens there. I have sold to Lewis the rest of the livestock and some of the furniture which will not fit into our new home, which is much smaller. I have kept our bed. Matthew and his father made it as a wedding gift, as well as the kitchen table and chairs that Matthew made.

President Lincoln went to Gettysburg to dedicate a national cemetery for the many Union dead who had fallen there. His speech has been widely recorded in the papers and as Matthew had before, I carefully cut a copy of it out of the local paper and placed it in a frame.

Four score and seven years ago our fathers brought forth, upon this continent, a new nation, conceived in Liberty, and dedicated to the proposition that all men are created equal.

Now we are engaged in a great civil war, testing whether that nation, or any nation so conceived, and so dedicated, can long endure. We are met on a great battlefield of that war. We have come to dedicate a portion of that field, as a final resting-place for those who here gave their lives, that this nation might live. It is altogether fitting and proper that we should do this.

But, in a larger sense, we cannot dedicate, we cannot consecrate we cannot hallow this ground. The brave men, living and dead, who struggled here, have consecrated it far above our poor power to add or detract. The world will little note, nor long remember what we say here, but it can never forget what they did here.

It is for us, the living, rather, to be dedicated here to the unfinished work which they who fought here, have, thus far, so nobly advanced. It is rather for us to be here dedicated to the great task remaining before us that from these honored dead we take increased devotion to that cause for which they here gave the last full measure of devotion that we here highly resolve that these dead shall not have died in vain that this nation, under God, shall have a new birth of freedom and that government of the people, by the people, for the people, shall not perish from the earth.

It was a profound speech in every way and one that I was sure Matthew would want to memorialize. In some small measure, it renewed my pride in the sacrifice that he was making. That we all were making.

As soon as the Christmas holiday is over, we will pack up the wagon and move. Fuller, as always, is a great help and Charlotte has lent him to me for a couple of days to help us get settled into our new home. Fort Gratiot is not far away and there is now a hospital there caring for the wounded who are returning from battle. My hope is that Kenneth and I may be able to find work there.

I as pack up the house, so many memories come flooding back to me, and it is hard not to be emotional about this change. Most of my children were born in this house. This was the last place I held Dickie and Cordelia. The last place I saw Matthew. This home has been a shelter and haven against the strife and anguish in the world all around us. Our home has always been a safe place. I know what I am doing is the best course. We can manage for much longer at the new house than we can here with the money we have. More importantly, we can find the work that we have no chance of finding here.

President Lincoln issued a Proclamation of Amnesty in which he offers pardon to those who participated in the current rebellion if they take an oath to the United States. He hopes that those in the border states who are tired of the fighting might lay down their arms and help to end this conflict. I do not know how successful that effort might be, but maybe it signals that progress is being made. Still, the columns of dead and captured memorialized in the paper continue to occupy more and more space, and grief and sorrow still run rampant through the country.

Finally, the day has come. It takes several hours to load up the two wagons and to get the livestock sorted. We will come back for the chickens in a few days. Lewis is coming tomorrow, and he will manage them till we return. Kenneth is still sullen but cooperative and Charles is excited about the change, as little boys often are.

"Mama, will I get to sleep in my own room in our new house?"

"No, you will have to share a room with your brother I'm afraid, but it is a very nice room with a window that looks out on the street. We are very close to the St. Clair River and you and Kenneth can go fishing there. Would you like that?"

"Can we Kenneth? Can we go fishing?"

"We sure can," replied Kenneth as he ruffled his brother's hair and smiled for the first time in many weeks.

We plodded along very slowly so that the cows could keep pace and it took the whole day to reach the new house, but we arrived just as the sun was going down. It took several hours for us to get everything out of the wagons and to get Moon and the cows settled in the barn. We would sleep on the floor tonight and work tomorrow to put together the beds. Charles slept with me while Fuller and Kenneth shared the bedroom.

"Fuller, I cannot thank you enough for all of your help," I said as he and I sat at the table having a cup of tea before heading off to bed.

"I am very happy to do it ma'am. I am very fond of Kenneth and Charles both, and I hope you will all be very happy here."

"I think you need to call me Millicent as we are friends now. You and I have been through so much together," I said smiling.

"Indeed, we certainly have Millicent," he replied.

"I just realized I don't even know your given name," I said.

"Edward, Edward Fuller. I was named after my great-grandfather."

"Thank you, Edward, for everything."

"We will miss seeing you at the house. I hope you will come to visit when you can and I'm sure Mrs. Whitsitt will stop and see you whenever she is in town," said Edward.

"I hope so. I know very few people in Port Huron, and I will very much look forward to her visits, and yours too?" I said hopefully.

"Of course, I will stop by to see if there is anything you need whenever I am in town," he replied with a shy smile.

As I sat here with Edward drinking tea, I realized how much I truly appreciated him. He had been so kind to me and helpful when Mariah ran away, and he searched diligently for Rebecca. He has been a father figure of sorts for Kenneth and Charles and there was no amount of thanks that would be adequate to show my appreciation. I turned down all but one lantern and suddenly realized there was a light that was sweeping through the house every minute or so, gently illuminating the ceiling and walls.

"Edward, what is that?"

He laughed softly, "It is the Fort Gratiot lighthouse. You are just on the edge of it, enough for the light to catch you as it sweeps the sea keeping the ships away from Point Edward."

I couldn't help but smile. A lighthouse to keep me from floundering on the rocks and to guide me home. It was a good sign.

Chapter Ten – *Andersonville*

The cold weather has been a bit of a blessing, providing us no excuse to avoid unpacking and placing everything just so. Once our things were in the house it began to feel much more like home. I made new curtains for the bedrooms, and it made the house very cheerful despite the gray gloom outside the windows. I enrolled Charles in the primary school at the end of the street, and he was able to walk back and forth with the other children who lived nearby. He and Kenneth were also making friends. People here knew nothing of Mariah or the Parkers and our relationship with them, so there was no judgment regarding our character which was a great relief.

The paper has reported that there has been a large escape of Union prisoners from the notorious Libby Prison. Apparently, they were able to dig their way out and 109 United States officers escaped. Though about half of them were later recaptured, the rest were able to make their way to Union encampments. This daring and relatively successful escape was by far the most dramatic of the war so far and it gave me some hope that Matthew might be able to join in that kind of effort.

February 1864

Dear Mrs. Wagner,

We are writing to inform you that your husband, Sargent Matthew Wagner of the Michigan 6th Calvary Company C, has been listed among those being held at Camp Sumter, Andersonville, Georgia.

I am sorry that my letter does not bring you better news, but know the United States Army and government are doing their utmost to recover all prisoners of war and to bring this conflict to a conclusion. There is no further status report as to his condition. You may communicate with your nearest Army office for additional reports as they become available.

Yours respectfully,

Lieutenant Albert W. Gordon

Michigan Calvary Regiment Assistant Commander

I'm relieved that I remembered to inform the Army of my new address and that mail has been sent to me here, but they write again to tell me nearly nothing. Now I know where he is but nothing about how he is, which is truly far more important to me than the former. I don't even bother to share this news with the boys as it will mean little to them. Kenneth reads through the weekly newspaper repetitively every evening. He looks for those kernels of information he thinks might give him some clues as to how the war is going, and more importantly when it might end.

More information is becoming known about the place where Matthew is now being held by a man who was able to escape, which is apparently a rare exception. Roughly 400 prisoners a day are arriving there as the Rebs continue to consolidate their prison camps. A stockade enclosed the place where the prisoners were held, but 19 feet inside the stockade was the so-called *deadline*. If a prisoner stepped into that deadline, the guards placed in watch towers were allowed to shoot them dead. Some walk into the deadline with intent when they can no longer bear the conditions in which they are held. There is a small creek running through the stockade for drinking and bathing, but it is regularly contaminated when rainwater runs from the area where the men defecate into the river. The men have no shelter from the cold, or the heat that will come this summer, except that which they can make from blankets or clothing. There are no fires with nothing to burn, so what little gruel they receive is eaten cold. Fuller was right. This really is hell on earth.

I have been able to obtain a position as a clerk at the hospital at Fort Gratiot which will pay me ten dollars a month and provide some food rations which will be very helpful.

Kenneth has found a job at the stable that Matthew had worked out of mucking stalls and cleaning tack. That will pay him two dollars per week. Charles is old enough now to manage at home after school by himself and the neighbor, Mrs. Chester, is there in case there is an emergency. He is often there playing with her son Harold, and so I do not worry about him.

I walk to work along the river each morning. While it is cold, there is a sense of accomplishment that we are providing for ourselves, and I enjoy the work although it is exhausting. Each morning the ships come bearing soldiers who have been wounded in the South as the Army distributes them throughout hospitals in the North. My assignment is the intake ward where the men first arrive and are evaluated for the care they might need. From there they are distributed to other wards within the hospital. Part of my job is to gather personal information for their record and then write to their families to inform them of their loved one's condition and location. It is odd now that my name will be the one at the bottom of the letter that a woman holds close to her heart, thanking God her husband is alive. Some men come with records from their prior hospital stays, but some come with very little.

"What is your name, soldier?"

"Hannibal West," the man said in a weak voice.

"What is your rank?"

"Private," he said.

"Where we you injured?"

"During the Mine Run campaign in Virginia, ma'am, some three months ago. I was in the hospital in Washington for a while."

"Is that where they amputated your arm?" I asked. A question I had asked so often now that it no longer caught in my throat.

"Yes."

"I see you are from Kalamazoo, Private West. Is that correct?"

"Yes, ma'am. I was born and raised there and enlisted from there in 1862," said Hannibal.

"How old are you, soldier?"

"I believe this is February so that would make me 19 ma'am," he replied with a slight smile.

"Is there someone you would like me to write to in Kalamazoo? Your parents perhaps?"

"Yes, please. My Ma and Pa if you would. I haven't learned to write yet with my left hand, but I am going to work on that," he said with a wry grin.

And so, the day went, making my list of people to write

to and some details about their loved ones before the men were moved on to various wards throughout the hospital. At night at the kitchen table, I would write the letters and put them in envelopes the Army had provided and bring them back with me the next day to be put in the post. When only a few men were coming in, I would sit in the wards and visit with some of the men to fill them in on the events of the day and try to ease their fears and homesickness.

"Kenneth, your fifteenth birthday is coming soon. Is there anything you would like to have?" I asked as we sat at breakfast on Saturday morning.

"I have a say in what I get?" he asked with surprise.

"Yes. I am not saying you will necessarily receive it, but I am asking if there is something you particularly want," I replied.

"Well, if I had my say I'd like to get one of those fishing nets," he said enthusiastically.

"We could get more fish with that!" said Charles adding his endorsement of his brother's proposal.

It seemed like a good idea. It was something he wanted and something that would likely result in more fish on the table. So that afternoon I made my way to the trading post next door to the bank. It seemed like they would be the most likely place to find this fishing net. As I turned onto the main street, I ran nearly head-on into a young woman hurrying in the opposite direction.

"Oh, I am sorry ma'am! I did not see you coming around the corner," she said as she grabbed my arm to keep us both from toppling over.

"Do not concern yourself. It was… Mariah?"

"Mother, what are you doing in this part of town?" she asked pointedly.

"We live here in town. Just down the way here, at the end of Elmwood Street. I saw you at Cordelia's burial. It was good of you to come," I said.

"Yes, Brooke got word to me. I was very sad to hear of her passing. You have sold the farm? What of the rest of the family? Father has returned?" she asked hopefully.

"Yes, I sold the farm and bought a small property here. No, unfortunately, your father remains a prisoner of war being held in Andersonville," I replied.

"My goodness," she gasped covering her mouth with her gloved hand. "Not Andersonville. I have heard the vilest things about that place."

"Sadly, yes. It's just Kenneth, Charles, and me here. Rebecca is living in a home for those who have mental illness in Detroit. Ultimately, we could not afford to stay on the farm. I'm working at the hospital and Kenneth is working at the stable."

Mariah just looked at me as if she was struggling to comprehend what I had said. I realized it was a lot to take in all at once. For us, the changes had come gradually. For her to learn all this at once truly had to be a shock.

"Rebecca is not mentally ill, is she?" she asked incredulously.

"She became much worse, Mariah. It was no longer safe to have her in the house. I did what I felt was best and she is well cared for."

"I see," she said after a moment.

"How are you and your son?" I asked finally.

"William is growing very quickly. He turned one just a couple of weeks ago and he is a happy and chubby little boy," she said smiling.

"I am glad to hear it."

"Mother, you could have come to me. I could have helped you stay on the farm. We have enough money."

"I want nothing to do with money that is earned through illicit means, and neither should you," I said vehemently.

"Well, I am sorry that you still feel that way, but I am happy with my choices and my life," she replied.

"It was good to see you, Mariah," I said.

"You too Mother. Give my love to Kenneth and Charles,"

she said as she nodded her head toward me before continuing on her way.

I stood there for another moment, gathering myself before I started back down the sidewalk toward the trading post. Mariah seems so grown-up. Her clothing and hat were very stylish, and her coat was trimmed with fur. My simple wool coat is shabby in comparison. But if the cost of staying on the farm was compromising my moral principles, I am glad I did not do it. Matthew certainly would not have approved if I had. The fishing net was two dollars, but it seemed like a good investment, and I knew Kenneth would be very happy. I made another stop at Cooks and picked up two hard candies, sugar, and a pair of new shoelaces for Charles' shoes. I also splurged on a new skirt for myself which was made of a beautiful wool fabric that would last me several years and keep me warm on my walks to the Fort.

Now that we live in town, we receive the news more regularly. We can even walk over to some of the store windows where they put the paper up so that you can read it from the sidewalk. As the war continues some Confederate prisoners have sworn their allegiance to the United States and joined the Union Army. Over 5,000 of them in the last few months. They have been organized into six regiments called the United States Volunteers but most call them Galvanized

Yankees. Several hundred of them had started the war as Union soldiers, but once captured they joined the Rebs, only to turn around and be captured by the Union. They were going to be charged as deserters but were spared if they enlisted in one of these new volunteer regiments.

In an odd twist, former Union soldiers who enlisted in the Confederate Army were also called Galvanized Yankees to identify them. Many German and Irish men who had been drafted by the Union Army joined the Rebs after they were captured rather than endure the conditions of the Confederate prison camps. It was clear that allegiances were not set in stone and men could change sides depending on their circumstances and what they thought would best serve them. That was hard for me to understand, but I have never been faced with the kinds of horror these men have. Perhaps I would do the same in their place.

April 1864

Dear Millicent,

I am pleased but surprised to be able to write you, but again quite skeptical that this will reach you. I hate to cause you pain, and I know I am causing you more worry, but I must speak honestly. Others must be told of the conditions here. Andersonville is a horrid place as I am sure you have heard. The stockade of hewn pine logs rises nearly sixteen feet high and cannot be breached. There are platforms on which the guards stand under a rough board roof. They are there to shoot any man who tries to cross the open space they maintain between us and the stockade, and they do it daily.

This place is the very essence of squalor and wretchedness. Many men are nearly naked, barefoot, and filthy in a way that cannot be truly understood until you see it with your own eyes. We make basic shelters by pinning together blankets or shirts to provide some protection from the rain and sun. Human excrement is everywhere, despite efforts to maintain clean areas, as many have diarrhea which they cannot control. The cold gruel they provide us once a day is barely enough to sustain us and scores are dying of malnutrition. The fleas feed on our bodies during the night and it is difficult to rid them from our clothes. Were most men to stand in the sun, they would not even cast a shadow, being so emaciated.

Many have dysentery and wounds quickly become gangrenous. The smell of this place is horrid and impossible to ignore. The dead, often in the hundreds each day, are dragged out to be buried in trenches but not before their clothes are scavenged by others, leaving them to be buried as they were born.

Share this letter, Millie, to anyone in the Army who will listen to our plight. We need to be liberated from this hell soon before we all perish. I am desperate to survive this place and come home. You are my whole heart, and my love for you and the children is all that sustains me.

Your husband,

Matthew

My heart broke for Matthew as I read his letter, but it also felt something else. Anger. Men, no matter their disagreements, should not be treated in this way. This is inhumane. War is a tragedy, war is bloody and brutal and horrid, but once captured, these men deserve to be treated as human beings. In Andersonville, they are being treated worse than most would treat their animals. No one leaves an animal to stand and sleep in its own waste. Why are these men expected to do so? A barely palatable gruel for their only meal each day? No. No, I cannot stand by and do nothing as Matthew and his fellow soldiers are treated in this way. I do not know what my course of action will be, but I will do what I can. Of that, I am sure.

As I lay in my bed that night watching the dance of the light from the lighthouse flickering across the ceiling, I cried for Matthew. I cried for all the men in prison camps tonight. On Sunday I will go and talk to Charlotte. She will know what to do. For now, I let my grief flow over me like a wave, and I did not resist it. It crashed across me over and over again, just like the ocean throws itself upon the rocks on the shore. But I would not wallow in this grief. My anguish helps no one, least of all Matthew. I will indulge it tonight, but tomorrow my sadness becomes action. I need to save my husband.

Chapter Eleven - *We All Must Fight*

I took the wagon by myself to see Charlotte. It was strange traveling down this road knowing I was not going to go home. It was stranger still to see others at my farm. I waved at Lewis before turning into the drive at Charlotte's house. I could not bring myself to stop, to see others living in the home I thought would be forever mine. It all seemed so surreal, and I did not want to endure it.

"Millicent, Mrs. Wagner, it is so very nice to see you," said Edward with a big smile.

"It is wonderful to see you too. How are you?" I asked as he took my coat.

"Very well thank you, was Mrs. Whitsitt expecting you? She did not mention you were coming."

"No, I did not have time to write but I need to speak to her about an urgent matter. Is she here?" I asked hopefully.

"Yes, she is here. I am sure she will be very happy to see you. Please, have a seat in the parlor and I will go and tell her you are here. I'll send Brooke in with some tea."

"Thank you, Edward," I replied as I watched him disappear into the kitchen.

Just a few moments later I could see him going up the

stairs. I hoped I was not disturbing Charlotte. Perhaps I should have written rather than showing up here unannounced. I was now starting to doubt the wisdom of my choice, but I felt a profound sense of urgency.

The sun was warm coming through the windows, and it glinted off the crystal and silver throughout the room. This house could not be farther from the grotesqueness and despair of Andersonville. The comfort and warmth I once felt here was now overshadowed by guilt and anxiousness and a need to do something, anything, to stop this suffering.

"Millicent, I am so happy to see you!" exclaimed Charlotte as she came into the parlor, and she embraced me immediately.

"I am very happy to see you too," I said with a weak smile.

"What is it? Fuller told me you need to see me urgently?"

"Yes, it's Matthew. I have heard from him, and I need your help," I said with a note of desperation as I handed her his letter.

"Of course, let me read this," she said putting on some glasses I had not seen her wear before.

I sat quietly waiting for her to read the letter, which she did, twice. Then she leaned back in her chair and closed her eyes. A tear leaked out from beneath her closed lids and trickled slowly down her cheek before falling off onto the chair. After a moment she opened her eyes and looked at me with a sadness I had never seen in her face before, even when we spoke of Leo or Deborah.

"Millicent, I am beyond aghast by Matthew's letter. I think we all know that conditions in the prison camps, in both the North and South are less than ideal… but inhumane? No, I don't think I would have expected to hear this kind of woeful tale, and it shakes me to my very soul. This… this is an abomination, and it cannot stand," she said finally.

I don't know why, but I began to cry again, perhaps just the relief of knowing that someone else was sharing my burden and that they felt as I did. That this could not stand. But would she know what to do?

"We need to go to Washington and speak directly to the Secretary of War Edwin Stanton," she said, rising from her chair and ringing for Fuller.

"Charlotte, I do not know if I can do that. I have a job now at the hospital and Kenneth is too young to be responsible for Charles for several days," I said my voice rising in a bit of a panic.

I desperately wanted to do something to make Matthew's plight known, but travel to Washington?

"Could we not just write a letter?" I asked hopefully.

"No, I don't believe that will be effective. If we are going to have a real impact, we need to see him in person," she replied, her hands on her hips.

"But how do we know he will even see us? We could go all that way and not even get past whoever it is that guards such places."

"He will see us. Edwin Stanton is an old friend of my husband. I will write him to let him know that we must speak to him. I am most certain that he will accommodate us," she replied confidently.

"But still, that doesn't solve the issue of my job or the boys."

"Fuller can go and stay with them while we are gone. Mrs. O'Connell and Brooke can manage here for a few days. I will speak to the person in charge at the hospital before we go and make sure it is sanctioned. I've no doubt when we tell him who we are going to see that he will permit you to be absent from your job, and he will probably still pay you!" said Charlotte.

"All right then. To Washington, we will go. If that is what is needed to help Matthew, then that is what shall be done," I said.

Charlotte was a force of nature the next few days preparing for our trip. I stayed with her while Edward stayed with the boys so that he could be in town to make the arrangements we needed for the train and a hotel in Washington. I had never stayed in a hotel before. I was not sure what to expect but Charlotte was reassuring. She also helped me pick out a few things from her wardrobe to wear and she gave me a nice valise to put them in. She also lent me a coat and two hats. Charlotte said that we needed to look like women of authority and means if we were going to be successful in trying to sway the Secretary.

Before we boarded the train three days later, I was able to talk briefly to the boys who were excited to have Edward staying with them.

"You mind Mr. Fuller now. I do not want to hear of any mischief while I am gone. Do you understand me clearly?"

"Are you going to be able to get Papa to come home?" asked Kenneth hopefully.

"I don't know about that darling, but we will do our best. At least we hope that the government is going to intervene to improve the conditions at the place where he is being held. Beyond that, we will see," I said as I kissed him on the cheek.

"You are coming back… aren't you, Mama?" asked Charles.

It nearly broke my heart to hear him ask that. Mariah, Matthew, Cordelia, Rebecca. I could understand why he might be afraid I might not return as his experience told him otherwise.

"I promise you, my son. I will return to you in just a few days," I said as I held him tightly to me.

"I love you, Mama," he said before he ran off to join Harold from next door on the walk to school.

When we boarded the train, my stomach flipped and flopped with a nervousness I don't think I had ever felt before. Who did I think I was putting on airs and going to see this important man in our nation's capital? I am no one. My husband is just one of thousands of men being so cruelly treated. Why would I think that he would pay any mind to me or my concerns?

"Every person has a right, no, a responsibility to speak up when they see injustice and inhumanity. If you do not, it is as if you support it or condone it. You allow it to continue to hide in the shadows rather than being exposed to the scrutiny of good men and women. Exposed for all to see," Charlotte said to me when I told her of my fear.

She was right, of course. To say nothing was a failure to act that I could not accept. I would never be able to live with myself if I did not try my very best to help my husband. Even if my efforts are for naught, I can go to heaven knowing that I was true to Matthew and my character to the end. We traveled along in relative silence as I watched out the window. The landscape changed more and more as we headed further south. We would travel all night, just stopping to exchange passengers and load more coal and water. Many of the cars were filled with soldiers being deposited at various locations along the track to Washington.

When we finally arrived the next morning, I was very tired, having slept little during the night. Charlotte on the other hand seemed to have slept soundly. I suppose she was used to this kind of traveling and she took it all in stride. Stepping off the train in Washington I was instantly more awake. The energy of this place was electric with people running to and from trains as if their very lives depended on it. Many armed soldiers walked up and down the train platform watching passengers arriving and departing. I wasn't sure if they made me feel safe or wary. A carriage was waiting for us, and the plan was to go directly to the President's House where Secretary Stanton had his office. As we rattled through the streets, I noted that some were dirt, some wood, and others paved with stone. The array of buildings was equally diverse. I was amazed at the number of very tall buildings but even more amazed at the fortifications and cannons that stood every few blocks. This city was impenetrable, as fitting the seat of the federal government I supposed. Along with cannons, there were hospitals, a great many hospitals. Outside each, you could see a few men in ragged uniforms smoking as they sat outside in the cold.

When we turned the corner, there in front of us was the President's House. It was grand indeed. I never imagined that I would be here and certainly not that I would be going inside. There were hay bales and fortifications all around the house, and guards stationed at short intervals, their weapons trained on the street. There were several carriages in front of us and we waited quietly in line for our turn to speak to the soldier at the gate. As people approached, he consulted some papers and either let the carriage pass or turned it away.

"Not to worry Millicent. They know we are coming, and we will be permitted to pass. I visited when President Buchanan was in office and it's all very grand, but we must remember why we are here. Do not let the glamour of this place blind you. These men are mere mortals just like us, despite what some of them might want you to think."

My cheeks turned red. Charlotte always seemed to know what I was thinking and so often it was my insecurity that she ferreted out. In my dreams I was more like her; sure of myself and confident. But truth be told, I was none of those things despite my efforts. We were indeed permitted to pass, but once inside the gate, the carriage was searched before we were allowed to pull up in front of the building. A man in a bright red coat opened the door, put down the stairs, and helped us out. A woman in a demure wool skirt and white blouse with a short jacket welcomed us and led us inside.

I could not help but gape at my surroundings, although in some ways it was less impressive than I had imagined. The woman explained that some of the artwork had been removed and was in storage to protect it in the event of a direct attack. There were soldiers and men in suits swarming through the halls in every direction, like so many ants at a picnic, one following another. We followed the woman to Secretary Stanton's office in the North Wing where we were seated on two leather chairs outside the door across from her desk. Men came in and out of the office every few minutes it seemed and each time we got a small glimpse inside.

I could see a large desk and a bespectacled man with a long brown beard streaked with white sitting behind it. He was often rifling through papers or gesturing with the cigar he held in his hand.

"Secretary Stanton will see you now Mrs. Whitsitt and Mrs. Wagner," said the woman as she came out of the office, leaving the door open behind her.

We rose from our chairs, and I followed Charlotte into the office. The woman closed the door behind us. There was another man there sitting on a couch, who rose as we entered. He was in uniform of some high rank it appeared. Although I must confess, I did not know the insignias well.

"Charlotte, my dear! How very nice to see you," said the Secretary as he came around the desk and kissed her on each cheek.

"The pleasure is all mine, Edwin. It's good to see you, although I wish it were under better circumstances," said Charlotte smiling at him. "May I present my dear friend, Mrs. Millicent Wagner," she said as she turned toward me.

"Mrs. Wagner, I am pleased to make your acquaintance. Please both of you sit down here," he said as he gestured toward two chairs directly in front of the desk. "Charlotte, I received your cable, and I've asked Brigadier General Richard Arnold to join us. He is my liaison regarding captured prisoners."

"Mrs. Whitsitt, Mrs. Wagner," the handsome General said as he nodded at each one of us in turn.

"My dear, how is Leo?"

Charlotte smiled, but you could see it was a sad smile and there was sorrow in her voice as she replied. "No better I'm afraid. The country has been good for me, but for Leo, there has been no improvement."

"Ah, I am most aggrieved to hear that. I was hopeful your

move would be just the tonic he needed," said the Secretary.

"So was I," she replied wistfully.

"Mrs. Wagner, I understand your husband is being held in Andersonville, and for that, I am most sorry," said the Secretary.

"Yes, sir. He has been held for a year and a half, roughly. This is his third prison as the Rebels have continued to move their prisoners further South."

"Indeed. They have many fewer men to fight than we do, and so it is imperative to them that they hold every soldier they can to try and improve their odds. But make no mistake, we are going to win this war and we are going to free all our prisoners," he said confidently.

"I understand you have a letter from Sargent Wagner. May I read it ma'am?" asked Brigadier General Arnold.

"Of course, sir," I said as I handed him Matthew's letter. I had been careful to bring it with me on this journey.

"Please, Richard, read it aloud," said the Secretary.

Charlotte and I sat there silently as he read the letter, and I noticed his deep baritone voice cracked several times while he was reading. I could feel the tears welling up in my eyes as I did nearly every time I read it, but I tried very hard to maintain my composure. This was not a time for tears.

"Mrs. Wagner, thank you for bringing this to me. I had no

idea conditions were this abhorrent. This is inhumane!" he exclaimed as he slammed his fist on the desk.

Charlotte and I both jumped slightly at the force of his anger, and I knew at once this was not a man whose displeasure I would want directed at me or my family. I was, however, heartened by the idea that this anger might be turned on those who tortured my husband and all our soldiers.

"General Arnold," he barked.

"Yes Mr. Secretary," he said snapping to attention.

"I want a full report on this Andersonville prison at once, and a plan for how to improve the conditions there. Or better yet, a proposal for how to get these men out of this hell," the Secretary bellowed.

"Ladies," he said as he nodded in our direction before quickly exiting the room.

"Thank you, Edwin," said Charlotte.

"Mrs. Wagner, you have my sincerest apology. I knew that the conditions in the Rebel prisons were abysmal but truly I had no idea it was this egregious. Thank you for coming all this way to bring this to my attention. I promise you that I will do everything in my power to try and rectify this situation. Truthfully, I would not be optimistic that they will release prisoners, and so I do not want to create false hope.

However, we will do what we can to make the conditions more livable for the men being held there."

"Thank you, Mr. Secretary. All I can hope for is that you will do what you can to help my husband and to help all the men being held there. I am most grateful for your efforts," I said as I reached over and squeezed Charlotte's hand.

"Thank you again, Edwin," said Charlotte as she rose from the chair.

"Of course, my dear, and give my best to Leo," he said as he once again kissed her on each cheek.

He then took my hand in both of his. "Mrs. Wagner, I owe you a debt of gratitude for both your husband's service and for your determination to help him and all the men who are suffering at the hands of the Confederates. We will defeat them."

"Thank you, sir. Truly, I thank you."

As we walked down the hall. a soldier came toward us in the narrow passage with his weapon held out in front of him vertically.

"Make way," he said.

Behind him was a tall thin man with a beard who I recognized immediately as President Lincoln. He walked quickly his head bowed slightly but you could see the consternation on his face. He looked tired and a bit gaunt. We pressed our backs against the wall to make space for the President to pass.

"Good afternoon, ladies," he said as he glanced up at us as he passed, going quickly into the Secretary's office we had just left.

Charlotte and I looked at each other and could not help but smile. I wonder what Matthew would think if he knew I had just been greeted by the President of the United States, one of the most powerful men in the world. With that, we left the President's House, boarded our carriage, and went to the hotel that Charlotte had arranged for us. I suddenly felt exhausted, as if all my strength had been drained. I could barely lift my arms. The hotel was very nice. It was well-furnished, comfortable, and not too far from the train station. I lay down on the bed and fell asleep immediately. It was nearly dark when I woke.

I freshened up and went next door to Charlotte's room, but there was a note on the door that she was downstairs. The hallways and stairs were covered in plush carpet, much like that in Charlotte's house, and the dark woodwork gleamed as if it had been polished just moments ago. At the bottom of the stairs was the main lobby. Just past the entrance was a small area of tables and chairs and I saw Charlotte there.

"Millicent, you are up! Are you feeling better?" she asked.

"Yes, much better thank you. I don't know why I felt suddenly so weak and tired, but the nap did me good," I said as I smiled at her.

"I'm just having some tea, but we can eat supper here if you are hungry."

"I am very hungry," I replied, realizing I had not eaten in some time. I had no appetite on the train.

"Wonderful! I am glad to hear it," she said as she smiled at me warmly.

"Charlotte, I cannot express to you how much your friendship has meant to me, but this… it is more than any friend should ever expect from another. You have been beyond generous in paying for this trip and in using your acquaintance with the Secretary to get me an audience with him. No matter what happens, whether he can help Matthew or not, I will rest easy knowing we have done everything that we could. Thank you is simply not enough but it is said with true sincerity and appreciation for you and everything you have done for me and my family. Not just today, but over the last two years. I don't know what I would have done without you."

"Millicent, I think of you as a sister, and I would do anything to help you and your family. It is my honor, truly.

Know that everything I do comes from a place of affection and care for all of you," she replied.

Together we enjoyed a lovely meal and talked endlessly about the people and things that surrounded us. Even the china and silverware were opulent! For dessert, we splurged on a lovely raisin and orange cake. Despite the war, the women were impeccably dressed, and the men were dashing in their uniforms and formal suits. It was, by a significant measure, the most dazzling experience I had ever had. For a few hours at least, I let myself enjoy something without feeling guilty.

As if Charlotte had not done enough, on our way home, we stopped in Detroit and visited Deborah and Rebecca. It was a joy to see her, and she seemed happy to see me, but she did not talk much. Neither did Deborah, but she was also very happy to see her sister and embraced her several times while we were there. Rebecca and I took a small walk around the garden, and I told her about our new house, my job at the hospital, and Kenneth's new fishing net.

"What about Cordelia? Does she miss me?" she asked.

I stopped dead in my tracks.

"Rebecca, remember that Cordelia died last year. We buried her next to Dickie. Kenneth and I were there with you," I said gently.

"I forgot, I guess," she said without emotion.

"Rebecca, my precious," I said as I hugged her close to me.

She did not resist but she did not hug me back. She just stood there with her arms at her sides, as if she were simply enduring my affection. It nearly broke my heart. We walked back to the building without speaking. Her only interest was the birds she could see flying through the garden. As we rode the remainder of the trip to Port Huron, I realized that Rebecca was in the very best place that she could be. It was a place where she could be kept safe and looked after. I don't know if you could say that she liked it there. I'm not sure she liked much of anything these days, but I knew now having seen her there that it was the right decision. Another thing to be grateful to Charlotte for. I don't know how I will ever repay her for all her kindness and financial support, but I would have to try and find a way.

Chapter Twelve - *Sorrow and Disappointment*

My walk to the hospital each morning is becoming a joy as spring is upon us once more. I enjoy the path that takes me along the river. The flow of men into the hospital has slowed some but continues at a steady pace. The young faces begin to blur one into another with the only constant between them being despair. They don't understand how they will manage in this world with less than they had when they came into it. I work now in one of the wards, helping to change dressings, writing letters for soldiers, or just sitting with them trying to provide some sense of comfort. I read from the paper or from books that have been donated to make a small library, and the men are very appreciative.

I have begun to think of these younger men as my children and the older ones as my brothers, and there is a genuine pain when one of them is lost. Sadly, that is a daily occurrence and while it has taken its toll on me emotionally, I would not trade this work for the world. In many ways, I feel as if I am caring for Matthew when I tend to them or read to them. I am doing for them what I would want someone to do for him if he were in their care.

It is odd to think of spring and not to be engaged in

tilling and plowing the fields. We have our small garden but even that is half of what we had at the farm and now we buy hay rather than grow it. City life has taken some getting used to, but I am most pleased that Kenneth and Charles have made friends, and to a smaller degree, so have I. When I take my lunch at the hospital my friend Susan and I sit together and talk about our children and the weather. Anything but the war, death, and dying. She lost her husband over a year ago at the Battle of Chickamauga, and she had one daughter who sadly also died that same year from influenza around the same time we lost Cordelia. These losses bond us and we share a comfortable friendship, each silently acknowledging the pain and loss of the other.

In the newspaper, they report that the government has begun sending supplies of clothing, blankets, and food to some of the worst prison camps. While this gladdens my heart, I wonder how much of the aid will make it to our soldiers. I've heard nothing more from Matthew or the Army in several months, but I no longer wait in line with the other women only to be told there is no news. Charles' birthday is in a couple of months, and I can think of no better present for him than for his father to come home.

As I approached the house on my way home from work, there was a carriage parked outside. I don't recognize it as

Charlotte's so I'm unsure who it might be, but I quicken my step. Could it be Mariah? Kenneth is waiting for me on the front porch.

"Who is here, my son?"

"Some men from the Army. I had them wait inside. I hope that is alright," he replied.

"Of course," I replied, hopeful that these men were bringing news from Secretary Stanton.

"Good afternoon, Mrs. Wagner," said the shorter of the two men who stood near the fireplace.

"Good afternoon. Have you brought me some good news from Secretary Stanton?" I asked as I removed my coat.

The two men looked at each other quizzically and I knew at once this was not the emissary I was hoping for.

"No ma'am. We are here on behalf of General Thomas W. Custer who leads the Michigan 6th Calvary. It is our sad duty to inform you that your husband, Sargent Matthew Wagner, is most recently reported among the dead, having perished while in captivity in Andersonville prison," the taller man said.

"You have our sincere condolences," said the shorter one.

I sat down in the chair. My mind whirled like the leaves on a windy fall day, spinning in circles. The soldiers stood there silently, their hats tucked under their arms, their backs straight as ramrods, the buttons on their uniforms shiny and new. Their trousers were creased, shoes polished and clean, their mustaches neatly trimmed, and their hair slicked back. I don't know why I was looking at them so intently, taking in every detail of how they looked. Perhaps it was to keep from my mind the vision of Matthew lying dead in the filth, being dragged naked to a trench to be buried in an unmarked grave. They stood there silently for several minutes that felt like hours, the only sound the ticking of the clock on the mantel.

"Mrs. Wagner, again, you have our sincere condolences. Now if you need nothing further, we will take our leave, ma'am," said the taller one.

"Yes, of course, thank you," I said not bothering to rise from the chair.

Kenneth closed the door behind him before running to me, throwing himself at my feet and burying his head in my lap as he grieved over the loss of his father.

"Where is your brother?" I asked.

"He is playing outside with that boy from next door," he replied.

"Go and fetch him but say nothing. I will tell him," I said. "Wash your face before you go."

As I waited for them to return, I wondered why I wasn't

crying. I've cried so many times these last couple of years for Matthew. How is it that I have no tears when I learn that he is not coming home, ever? How am I going to tell my little boy that his father is gone? I am grateful that Kenneth was here, so I did not have to tell him, but Charles is the one who is always the most hopeful and the surest that his father is coming back to us. Now I must take from him the dream he has carefully nurtured these many months.

"Mama," said Charles as he ran to me smiling. He hugged me tightly.

"My darling little boy," I said as I took his dirty hands in mine.

"Kenneth said you need to talk to me. Am I in trouble?" he said with consternation.

"No, you are not in trouble. We have some news about Papa. Some Army men came to see me today. They told me that he died. I'm sorry Charles, but Papa won't be coming home after all. He's in heaven now with Cordelia and Dickie."

"No, that's not fair!" he screamed as he stomped his foot, tears already streaming down his face, before running off to his room and slamming the door behind him.

"I'll go, Mother," said Kenneth.

I leaned back in the chair. It started slowly, the way a pot does on the stove. Bubbles rise from the bottom to break on the surface, increasing in size and number until the white foam rises from the pot, and spills out onto the stove, hissing and spitting. So, it was with me until the tears spilled out onto my cheeks, running down my face, till they dripped off to fall onto my lap below. There was no sound, just the tears one after another in a steady stream until there were no more. It was dark by the time I could rise from the chair, stiff from having sat so long in one position. I went to check on the boys and found them together, both curled up in Kenneth's bed, sound asleep.

I sat down at the kitchen table and wrote letters to Charlotte, Bessie, and Shubal. I would write a letter I could deliver to Mariah. Maybe now I would consider moving back to New York. While I wanted to visit Rebecca, I am not sure the visits are of much importance to her. Would she really miss me if I did not see her again? I do not want her to feel as if I have abandoned her. For now, I think it is best to do nothing. We are comfortable here and the boys are settled so maybe the best course of action is no action at all. It all seems rather… anticlimactic. I thought if this was my fate that somehow the world would be turned upside down when the news came. Perhaps we had already done so much by selling the farm and moving to town that the world has already changed and can change little more now.

As the weeks go by, we all seem to be moving past our loss. The boys seem to be once again carefree and into their normal mischief. Kenneth spends more and more of his free time away from home with his friend Patrick. I don't know where the boys go or what they are doing, but if there is no trouble, I do not mind. Matthew was about his age I think when he started working full-time on his father's farm. He was able to attend school a bit longer than Kenneth has, but he is a smart boy and I do not expect that to become an impediment. It appears he intends to follow in his father's footsteps to become a blacksmith. I wish so much we had Matthew's things as all those necessary tools will need to be repurchased at quite a cost.

For Charles' birthday, I gave him a new fishing rod, and Kenneth purchased with his own money a small pocketknife for his little brother. Charles was very happy, and we enjoyed his favorite meal that day as well. I made chicken and dumplings with an apple pie.

"Mother, there are letters for you in the post," said Kenneth as he set two envelopes on the kitchen table.

One from Bessie, which I opened first, shared the sad news that our father has died from old age. While I loved my father, I will not grieve for him as I did my mother as he and I were truly never close. She has once again extended an invitation for us to come and live with her especially now that father is gone. Her husband died many years ago and all but one of her children are no longer living at home. The other letter was from Charlotte, inviting us to all come for the weekend and enjoy the lake and the grounds. It would be a nice change for the children. I haven't seen Charlotte since we returned from Washington, but we do write regularly.

"Mama, I would rather stay here in town for the weekend while you and Charles go to visit. May I?" asked Kenneth.

"What will you do with your time?"

"I plan to work for a few hours on Saturday, but then Patrick and I would like to go to the fair that is in town if that would be alright?" he replied hopefully.

"Oh yes, I heard about that when I was at Cook's a few days ago. Yes, you may go with Patrick. I will leave you one dollar to spend for your amusement and food. If you wish to spend more than that, it will have to come from the part of your money that is set aside for pocket change. There is to be no smoking or drinking of any kind. Is that clear?"

He nodded his understanding and hugged me before heading out the door, I'm sure to find Patrick. Charles was equally excited to be going to Charlotte's house. He enjoyed Fuller's company very much and, in some ways, I could see that Fuller treated him as he would his own son if he had one. Edward had never married and had no children, but I know not why. He seems that he would be a good husband and father, but perhaps he had no interest in either, although he is very good with both Kenneth and Charles.

Kenneth put Moon on the wagon for me before leaving for the stable. Charles is now able to climb in on his own without being lifted. The two of us ride along as he tells me all about his days at school and we sing a few songs his teacher has taught them. I no longer cringe so much as the farm comes into view. Now that the knowledge that Matthew is not coming home has been cemented, I am further confirmed in my decision. Lewis and his wife have had another child, which Charlotte wrote to me about. They seem very happy on the farm of which I am very glad. It's what Matthew would have wanted too.

"Millicent so good to see you," said Edward as he opened the door, not even pretending this time to try and call me Mrs. Wagner. Of course, he could only be so familiar when Charlotte was not in the room although I'm sure she would also not mind if he was doing so at my behest. He ruffled Charles' thick brown hair.

"Young man, I believe that Miss Brooke has some cookies and milk for you in the kitchen if you go that way, no doubt."

"Thank you!" he shouted as he ran quickly in that direction.

I could not help but laugh. It felt good to laugh. I needed to do more of it.

"You know your way to the parlor, Millicent. I'll bring the tea in a moment. Mr. and Mrs. Whitsitt are expecting you," he said quietly.

"Leo is downstairs?" I asked, quite surprised.

"Yes, he wanted to meet you, but he is still not well. He is quite frail, I'm afraid. I don't know how much longer he can go in this way. The doctor is here every few days," he said with genuine sadness.

When I walked into the parlor, a man was sitting in a wheelchair near the window, his back to the door. Even from the back, you could see that he was frail. He was bent forward slightly with his gnarled hands resting on the arms of the chair. He wore a heavy sweater and a blanket over his legs, although it was not cold in the house and the sun was quite warm coming through the windows. I looked about but did not see Charlotte and wondered if I should wait.

"Char?" said a gravelly voice coming from the man in the chair.

He must have heard my footsteps or the rustling of my skirt.

"No, Mr. Whitsett. It is Mrs. Wagner, Millicent," I said as I walked across the carpet to stand next to his chair.

"Ah, Mrs. Wagner. I thought you were my wife," he said as he turned his head slightly to look up at me.

His eyes were very blue and watery with age, his face heavily lined with many brown discolorations on his very fair skin. His hair was quite thin and what he did have was very light, almost white.

"Did you need me to find her?" I asked anxiously.

"No, no, my dear. Pull up a chair, just there," he said gesturing toward a small chair next to the credenza. I brought it over and sat it close so that I could sit facing him.

"I am glad you have come. I was looking forward to meeting you after all this time. My wife talks of you frequently, and very fondly. I have appreciated your friendship toward her and thank you for it," he said punctuating his sentences with coughing.

"Well, I am very happy to meet you, but you certainly do not need to thank me. If anything, I am the one that owes both you and your wife my thanks. Charlotte has done so much for me and my family. I will be forever grateful and forever in your debt," I replied sincerely.

"Oh, my dear, the things that are done with money, by those that have it, are less meaningful than the things that are done by the heart that cannot be purchased. True friendship is one of those things," he said with a slight smile.

I could only smile and nod. The generosity of these two people was more than I have ever encountered in my life. It is such a shame that they have no surviving children as I'm sure they were wonderful parents.

"I am aggrieved to hear of the loss of your husband, Mrs. Wagner. This war is like a monster that is not satisfied unless it devours the very best of what this country has to offer. To die on the battlefield is honorable to be sure, but to die in the filth and agony of a prison camp is valiant. One must be heroic to have the will to survive that kind of place for even one day, let alone the many, many months your husband did. You should be very proud of him. I am sure he wanted nothing more in this life than to return to you and his children," said Mr. Whitsitt.

"Thank you, Mr. Whitsitt. I had never really thought of it in that way," I said quietly.

"Leo, please," he said as he reached over and patted my hand.

"Of course, if you wish, and please call me Millicent, or Millie," I responded.

"Millie. That fits you, I think. You know Millie, your husband is not the only one who has been heroic these many months. You have been as well. You have faced many difficulties during his absence… Mariah's betrayal, Cordelia's passing, Rebeca's departure, selling the farm, and of course your husband's suffering and death. Charlotte has told me about all that fate has dealt you. Dealing with each of these things was your own act of valor and courage. It is easy for one to lie down and simply give up when life overwhelms you, but you did not do that. You fought back, for yourself and your children and you, my dear, are to be commended."

I could feel myself blushing. Certainly, I did not deserve this praise. What Matthew and others like him have endured is worthy of recognition, but what I have done is what any woman would have done, wasn't it? He looked intently at me with those piercing blue eyes.

"It is hard to sit here, waiting to die, as I do every day. But it is easy compared to choosing to fight back, choosing to live. Keep up that fight Millie, and you will someday find happiness again. I am sure of it," he said just as Charlotte joined us.

"Millicent, I didn't realize you were here! I'm so sorry to have kept you waiting, but it looks like my husband has been entertaining you," she said as I rose to embrace her.

"Yes, he has," I replied as I reached over and squeezed his hand smiling at him.

This weekend brought to my soul a lightness I had not felt in some time, perhaps since Matthew left. I played what Leo had said to me over and over in my mind. The idea that I needed to be commended was a foreign one. I have heard of a few women, unable to manage without their husbands, who abandoned their children to orphanages and left to start a new life in a new place. That is the kind of person I could never be, and would never want to be, but I can understand it too. The feeling of being overwhelmed, of not having the strength to go on, the pain of facing the things you would rather not face. There were many nights I laid alone in our bed thinking maybe the children would be better off with someone else, that maybe I wasn't strong enough to manage everything, especially Rebecca. Would Mariah have left us as she did if I had been a better mother? But I concluded that despite my insecurities and frailties, which are many, my place is with my family. To do whatever I can, imperfect as it may be, to be the wife and mother my family needed. And yes, I am proud of myself. Proud for not running away and not giving up. I am proud because I kept trying and did my best.

We had a wonderful time at Charlotte's house. I wish that we were closer to each other again, but there is no way I can live that far from town with my job at the hospital. I don't know how long it will last. Surely when the war is over, at some point, we will not be needed. For now, the work is meaningful to me, and the pay and rations are necessary. With Kenneth contributing most of his wages to the household, I can meet our monthly needs without dipping into the monies from the sale of the farm. I do use it for extra things like the fish net and fishing rod. All in all, we are doing well… better than some, worse than others, which is the place I have been fortunate to be in most of my life.

When we arrived at the house it was nearly dusk but there were no lamps lit and Kenneth was not home. In fact, it looked like he had not been there since we left. Perhaps he had decided to stay with Patrick? Surely, he would be home later since he must work tomorrow. A light supper was all that Charles and I needed, having consumed a plentiful lunch before departing for home. But as the hours ticked by, I began to worry. It was nearly nine and there was still no sign of Kenneth. The yellow house on the corner was where Patrick lived with his mother. I decided to walk down and see if Kenneth was there, or if Patrick knew where he might be.

"Charles, I'm going to go down the street to see if Kenneth is at Patrick's house, so if you get up and I'm not here, don't worry. I'll only be gone a few minutes," I said as I tucked him into bed.

"Alright, Mama. Night," he said as he snuggled down into

his blankets.

"Good night," I said kissing his forehead.

The lantern lit the street and cast shadows upon all the little houses that lined the block. At this time of night, nearly everyone was asleep as the days start early and are long and laborious. I saw no one as I made my way to the corner, save one stray dog who decided he would accompany me.

"Hello there. Do you belong to someone around here or are you just wandering?" I asked the scruffy fellow.

A tail wag was all I got in return, which frankly was more than I had expected. I continued to talk to him as we walked and he stayed with me, even lying down to wait while I went up to the door. There was a light on, so hopefully I would not be waking anyone. I knocked on the door lightly and it opened immediately.

"Patrick, where have you been?" said the gray-haired woman as she opened the door.

"No, I'm sorry. I'm Mrs. Wagner, from the end of the block. My son Kenneth was going to the fair on Saturday with Patrick, but I have just returned home, and he is not there. Do you know where the boys are?"

"Oh my. No, please come in Mrs. Wagner. I am at my wit's end, and I have no idea where the boys are," she said as she lit another lamp.

"When was the last time you saw them?" I said, starting to feel equally concerned.

"Patrick and Kenneth were here mid-day on Saturday. They had something to eat before they headed over to the fair. I went to the fair myself later and I saw them playing one of the games and they assured me they would be home later, but Patrick never came home. I assumed they were at your house, but when Patrick did not appear today, I knew something was wrong."

"Have you looked around town for them?" I inquired.

"As best I could. I have a little girl, Kate, who is ten. I asked at all the stores and of those I encountered on the sidewalk, but no one remembered seeing them since Saturday."

"I also have a younger child; my son Charles is sleeping at home so I cannot stay long. There is no use looking in the dark. I'll come in the morning, and we can go together to the stable and the Deputy Constable's office and see what they can do to help us," I said hopefully.

"I agree. Thank you, Mrs. Wagner. I will see you in the morning."

"I'm so sorry. I forgot to ask your name," I said awkwardly.

"Oh goodness me! I am so flustered. I am sorry. Marie,

Marie Dutton," she replied with a nervous laugh.

"Marie, I am sure the boys are fine and are just being a bit irresponsible. I doubt very much they will both miss work tomorrow," I said reassuringly.

"Probably so. Patrick loves his job at the stable and I know Kenneth does too. That's all these boys talk about when they are together is horses and tack. Heck, they are probably staying at the stable for all we know," she said optimistically.

"Probably so. Goodnight, Marie," I said as I made my way off the porch to find the dog still there waiting on me.

"Well, here we are once more," I said in response to the wagging tail. The dog walked beside me again all the way back to the house as if it were his mission to accompany me. When I reached the house, it was clear he wanted to come in.

"Now, this is where we will have to part company, I'm afraid. I will get a little something for you to eat."

I barely slept during the night, anxious to find Kenneth in the morning. Charles did not comment on Kenneth's absence, and I thought it best not to bring it up since he did not. When I opened the front door, the dog was still there. He had been lying up against the door all night it seemed.

"Hello," said Charles as he scratched the top of his scruffy head.

"Charles don't touch him. He needs a bath. He's very dirty."

"Can we keep him?" he asked expectantly.

"No, we can't keep him. He probably belongs to someone, and he will find his way home eventually," I replied firmly.

I dropped Charles next door on my way down the block so he could walk to school with Harold. I passed a little girl coming out of Marie's house who I assumed was her daughter Kate.

"Good morning," she said cheerfully as she walked past, apparently unaware of the drama playing out with her brother.

Marie and I walked quickly and mostly silently over to the south side of town. The doors of the stable were open, and we walked into the stalls, but we did not see anyone there except a half dozen horses. We walked through to the forge in the back and there was one man there stoking a fire.

"Excuse me. We are looking for Kenneth Wagner and Patrick Dutton," I said.

"Well, that makes two of us my dearie. Those rascals haven't shown up for work today," he said with something that almost sounded like a growl. He chewed on a piece of straw as he talked to us, his hands and clothes covered with the soot that comes from working in the forge. I knew it well. The smell of the place was familiar, the same way Matthew always smelled when he had been shoeing.

"When was the last time you saw them?" asked Marie.

"They were here on Saturday morning, but I've not seen them since then," he said as he threw another log and worked the bellows to stoke the fire.

"Thank you," I said as we turned to go.

"Tell them to get in here pretty quick if they want to keep their jobs. Otherwise, I'll find me a couple of new hands. Won't take me no time at all," he said as he spit his straw onto the ground.

We walked even more quickly to the Constable's office. My heart was starting to beat a bit faster. Perhaps some calamity had befallen them. There can be some very unsavory people who follow these fairs around from town to town. By the time we reached the office, I could feel my hands starting to shake.

"Good morning, ma'am. Can I help you?" said the young man at the desk near the door.

"Yes. We are looking for our sons. Their names are Kenneth Wagner and Patrick Dutton," I said.

"Oh, I can help you with that. Follow me, ladies," he said as he unlocked a heavy door, pushing it open and gesturing inside. There on a jail cell bench sat our sons.

"What is going on here?" asked Marie.

"These men have been arrested for stealing. They took a strong box by force, containing nearly forty dollars from a vendor at the fair early Sunday morning. Fortunately for us, and unfortunately for them, the man they stole from was able to describe them. We found them later in the day trying to spend some of the money."

All the pride and sense of accomplishment I had been feeling yesterday now vanished. My son sat in jail for stealing. Perhaps it's a good thing that Matthew isn't here to see this. I'm sure his disappointment would be most profound… but certainly, no more than my own.

Chapter Thirteen - *Do I?*

Kenneth had no explanation for his behavior other than the impulsiveness that young boys often feel. I sense that Patrick was the instigator and being a few years older he will pay a bigger price. Marie and I were there in court the day the boys were sentenced for the crime they committed. Patrick received one year in the county jail and Kenneth, because he was only sixteen, received nine months in the Michigan Reform School in Lansing. The man we had met at the stable was also in court when the boys were sentenced. He spoke on their behalf, even offering to rehire them if he had a need when they were released, which was very kind of him and probably more than they deserved.

We did get a chance to say goodbye before Kenneth boarded the train. He was remorseful, and while I appreciated his repentance, it did me little good. Now we had only one income to rely on, but one less mouth to feed so perhaps it will be alright. Honestly, I do not know. Poor Charles… another loss to bear. Even though I assure him his brother will return early next year it does little to assuage his fears. I also told him his father was coming back so I could understand why he would doubt me. When I went through

Kenneth's things to gather his clothes for washing, I found a bracelet. I am sure it is the one that went missing from Cooks store. The next time I was in the store I would leave it discreetly on the counter and address it with Kenneth when he returned.

It was impossible now to consider going to New York. We would have to stay here at least until Kenneth was released. More shame on me and my family. First Mariah, now Kenneth. I am looking forward to being able to leave this town for a new start in New York where people know none of this.

I focus on work and spending time with Charles. He feels so lonely now as he grew up in a house filled with brothers and sisters and now has none. Maybe I need to consider trying to make amends with Mariah so that he could spend time with her and her son. I just feel so torn regarding the whole thing. To patch things up with her is to acknowledge that I accept what she did, what she is doing, and I don't know if I can do that, even for Charles. Had she not left us, we might have been able to manage on the farm even without Rebecca. Even if she had married Jeremiah, his family would have helped us, and we would still be on the farm. But I realize I must stop trying to relive the past. It does none of us any good and we need to look to the future. There is still a great deal of life ahead of us, ahead of me, and we need to live it as those we have lost would want us to do.

The hospital has in some ways become a haven for me. I so enjoy spending time with the soldiers. Susan and I enjoy each other's company. She has come to the house for dinner a few times and we will be going to her home next week.

"Millicent, how lovely to see your beautiful face this morning," said Lieutenant Wilson.

"Good morning, Lieutenant. You seem especially chipper. You had a good night I take it?"

"I did, for the first time in many months I slept with very little pain in the leg which is not there. Such an odd thing to say, really," he said with a smile.

"Yes, I suppose it is. The doctors call it phantom pain. You feel the pain in a limb that isn't there, but I do know it gets better," I said as I fluffed up his pillow and helped him to sit up in his bed.

"I'm going to get out of here soon, I'm sure of it," he said as I sat down next to his bed to change his dressing.

He was probably right. His wound had healed well, and he was walking sufficiently with his crutches. I would miss him. He has always been very optimistic and kind, especially when he heard of my own loss from one of the other nurses.

"Millicent, I want to ask you something. It's important.

Can you stop for a moment?"

I looked at him expectantly.

"Millicent, can you move your chair a bit closer please?" he asked as he gestured for me to move nearer to the head of his bed.

"Ah, much better. Now…" he said taking my hand in his, "You know I have grown very fond of you, and I would like to marry you as soon as I get out of this place. Please tell me you would do me the honor of becoming my wife," he said with the utmost sincerity looking directly into my eyes without so much as a blink.

I was shocked for a moment. Perhaps he was joking, and he was expecting me to laugh? But then, I could see he was sincere. I needed to respond carefully as I did not want to do anything to hurt his feelings.

"Richard, I am beyond flattered by your offer, but truly we know very little about each other beyond what we have said to one another here during your care. How can you know that I would make you a good wife?"

"You are kind, good-hearted, beautiful, and generous. Those are the qualities that I think are necessary for a good wife. I know you might be worried that I would not be able to support you given my condition, but my father owns an accounting firm in St. Clair Shores, and I will return to work there. They also have a lovely home with plenty of room for us that I will inherit. You will never want for anything."

"Richard, I don't know what to say. Truly, it is very kind of you," I replied with a slight smile.

"If you say yes, you will make me the happiest man on earth and I will do my best to make you the happiest woman," he said as he kissed my hand. I blushed and looked around to see if anyone was watching, but everyone seemed to be going about their own business while paying us no mind.

"I will consider your offer, truly. But for now, I must get this dressing changed as I have other patients to attend to, and I can't spend my whole day here with you," I said with a wink.

"Oh, if only you could," he said wistfully before throwing his arm over his eyes and pretending to be wounded in his heart with a great deal of drama. He made me laugh despite myself.

As I walked home that evening along the river I thought about Richard. He was a handsome man, a few years younger than me, his family is from just south of here so we would stay in this general area. In fact, I would be even closer to Rebecca. He knew about Mariah and Kenneth through our conversations, and it seemed it did not impede him. I was sure, based on what I did know of him, that he would be a good father to Charles and Kenneth. While I was fond of him certainly, I did not love him as I had Matthew when we married, but was that necessary to be happy?

Life would certainly be much easier with a man earning a good living. I knew my job would end soon, forcing me to find some other work, which would not be easy. When the war did finally end, men would be returning and some of the jobs now being done by women would be taken back by the men who needed them, with no consideration for the women who also required the income. This is not a society that works well for unmarried women, and it was not something I was going to be able to change. I had to find my way as best I could.

Charlotte would be a good sounding board. She always seemed to have a salient point of view on nearly everything and she was not reluctant to share it, which I always appreciated, even the few times we have not agreed. The Lieutenant would be in the hospital for a few more weeks I'm sure, so perhaps I had a bit of time to understand where my heart and mind truly are. But, before I could even think about my own situation, there was another to face. I received word that Leo had died. I needed to get to Charlotte now.

Hitching Moon to the wagon alone was not easy but I

managed by standing on a milk crate. I decided it would be best to leave Charles here and Mrs. Anderson next door was gracious enough to keep him for a few days. Her son, Harold, is his best friend. He also needs to be in school and with someone with whom he is comfortable instead of having to deal with more loss. Although he did not know Leo, the mood would be a solemn one. It would be best to avoid that for him if I could. Driving out to the house it began to rain. It was one of those summer showers that started and stopped quickly but even still I was soaked to my skin and had dried little by the time I arrived.

"Millicent, what in heaven's name," said Edward as he opened the door.

"I know I must look a fright. There was a heavy rain just after I left town. I am soaked and so are my clothes," I said, trying to make light of my damp circumstances.

"Well, you could never look a fright, but I am sure you would like to get out of those clothes. Why don't you go straight upstairs? You will be staying in the room you were in before, the one on the left. Mrs. O'Connell is upstairs, and she can lend you a hand with anything you might need. Or I can send Brooke up if you prefer?"

"Oh no Edward, I couldn't. I need to pay my respects to Charlotte first," I replied.

"No need, she has gone out to the undertaker in Wales and will not be back for a bit. I am very confident she would not want you to sit in these wet clothes until then," he replied.

"She went to Wales by herself?"

"No, Mr. Whitsitt's brother arrived a few days ago. She had sent for him when it became clear that he did not have much time. They have gone together to make the necessary arrangements. There has been some discussion as to where his final resting place should be and the ride will give them a chance to talk," said Edward closing the door behind me.

"Now, upstairs. Please, Millicent, before you become ill," he said with a smile.

"Thank you, Edward, as always," I said gathering up my wet skirts to ascend the stairs. I could feel the water squishing in my shoes.

Edward was right. Despite the warm summer air, I was chilled in these wet clothes, and I was relieved to get out of them. I had only one other dress with me so it would have to do.

"Mrs. Wagner, tis good to see you again my dearie," said Mrs. O'Connell as she came into my room.

"It is good to see you too Mrs. O'Connell. I wish it were under better circumstances," I said as I returned her hug.

"Ah yes, Master Leo was a fine man to be sure, but I thank the Lord that he is no longer suffering and that he has now gone to his final reward. He was a good man, and I will miss him," she said as she wiped away a small tear.

"Will you find new employment now?" I said as I began peeling off my wet garments.

"Thankfully no, Mistress Charlotte has asked me to stay on. I've always helped her to dress and with her hair and such things when I wasn't tending to Master Leo. I'll stay on and pick up a few chores that Brooke would normally have done. I do love it here, and this is the closest thing I have to a family this side of the pond, you know," she said as she helped me peel off my stockings.

"I'm glad you'll be staying," I said as shook out the dress I removed from my bag.

"I hope you don't mind me saying so, Mrs. Wagner, but I think you might feel a bit, shall we say, out of place in that dress. The people who will be coming for the wake will be high society, don't ya know, and they will all be in their fancy black dresses."

"But this is the only black dress I have. I didn't bring anything else other than what I was wearing," I said rather mortified.

"Ah, you leave it to me. Go on into the washroom and

clean up a bit and I'll be back in a moment, don't you fret," she said as she patted me on the cheek.

Mrs. O'Connell reminded me of my mother, and I often felt like she was talking to me as a daughter when I was here. It was a comforting feeling, and I was very glad that she would continue to be here whenever I would visit.

"Here," she said as came into my room carrying a black dress. "This belonged to Miss Deborah, and she was very close to your size. I am sure Mistress Charlotte would be happy to have you wear it."

"Oh no, Mrs. O'Connell. I couldn't wear it, at least not without talking to Charlotte first," I said with chagrin.

"Talk to me about what?" I heard from behind me.

"Oh, Charlotte!" I said as I turned to embrace her. "I was so sorry to hear about Leo's passing."

"You are a dear for coming so quickly. I'm very glad you are here. Now what is it that we need to talk about?"

Mrs. O'Connell quickly filled her in on my situation and Charlotte couldn't help but laugh as she looked at me standing there, in my undergarments, my hair still wet and stringy.

"Millicent, I don't know why it did not occur to me before, but I have many things that once belonged to Deborah that she can no longer wear or have. By all means, avail yourself of anything you might need, and you should keep what you like."

"Charlotte I couldn't. Your generosity has already been overwhelming," I said as I could feel the hot sting of tears welling up in my eyes.

"Now Millicent, do not cry as I will join you, so please let me do this for you. These things are of no use to Deborah, and they should be given a new life through you. Mrs. O'Connell, I think there are some undergarments in that closet as well and several pairs of shoes. Would you see what else you can find?"

"At once," she said smiling as she left the room.

When she returned, she had armfuls of lovely clothes. Together we picked out one of the three black dresses, beautiful silk undergarments, and shoes. All were a perfect fit. Then we tackled my hair, pinning it up with some lovely clips, and just leaving a few cascades of curls down the back. As I stood looking at myself in the mirror, I felt such conflicting emotions. I was here for Leo's wake after all, but this was the most beautiful and glamorous I had ever looked, excepting our trip to Washington. The dress had layers of black netting under fine silk bustled at the back with a large bow. The petticoats held the dress out wider than anything else I had ever worn. The long sleeves were adorned demurely with black covered buttons from wrist to elbow where they were met with two rows of ribbons. The bodice was beautifully trimmed in black lace and formed a point at the skirt of the dress.

Finally, I felt presentable, and as I made my way carefully down the stairs, I found Edward in the foyer having just answered the door. When he looked up at me, I saw something in his face I had never seen before. A genuine affection softened his eyes as he watched me descend.

"Millicent, I know this may be inappropriate, but I have to say you look beautiful," he said shyly.

"Thank you, Edward," I said as I felt the heat rising in my cheeks.

"Mr. Whitsitt is laid out in the parlor so you will be in the formal parlor this evening. Let me show you the way," he said as he gestured down the hallway next to the stairs.

This part of the house was unknown to me, and I gathered from prior visits that these were rooms that were seldom used. When Charlotte and Leo built this house, I'm sure they thought he would get better, that there would be parties and a steady stream of visitors. Sadly, that was not what happened, and the smaller receiving parlor had always sufficed. This room was twice as large with a grand piano in one corner and a very large fireplace that held a small fire to ward off the evening chill. Half a dozen overstuffed chairs and tables with three sofas formed several vignettes of furniture to facilitate conversation. There were two large tables under the front windows filled with food. Meats, cheese, nuts, fruits, and large vases of fresh flowers were everywhere. On another table sat beautiful cut crystal glasses and several decanters of dark liquid I could only assume was whiskey or brandy. There were also several bottles of wine and some other spirits I did not recognize.

Suddenly, I wished Edward were not leaving my side. There were at least seven people in the room including Charlotte and I felt a bit overwhelmed.

"You will be fine, just be yourself," he whispered. "Mrs. Wagner," he said in a louder voice before turning and leaving the room.

"Millicent, let me introduce you to everyone," said Charlotte as she came over and took my elbow. "You look lovely my dear. That dress is a perfect fit," she said quietly as she steered me toward the distinguished men standing near the fire.

"Millicent, let me introduce you to my brother-in-law Joshua Whitsitt, and his son, Alan. This is my dear friend Mrs. Millicent Wagner."

"It's a pleasure to meet you. I am very sorry for your

loss," I said to each man in turn.

"Mrs. Wagner," said Joshua in a booming baritone.

If Leo's voice had been more robust, I'm sure the two men would have sounded very much alike with something similar about their accents.

"Charlotte has told me all about you during our time together today. You also have my sincere condolences on the loss of your husband. Know that the Union appreciates his sacrifice, and yours," he said as he raised his glass to me.

"Thank you," I replied.

"Mrs. Wagner, it is a pleasure to meet you. I work in the office of the Army Command in Washington, and I heard about the visit you and my aunt made to see Secretary Stanton. He spoke very highly of you and your dedication to bringing to his attention the plight of our soldiers being held in those horrid Rebel prison camps," said Alan.

"Thank you, but it is praise I do not deserve I am afraid. It was no more than any woman would do, given the opportunity I am sure," I replied demurely.

"Not at all, Mrs. Wagner. You gave your husband a voice when he did not have one. Although he did not survive the horrors of that place, there may be many others who will because of your efforts."

My heart swelled, not with pride, but with a feeling of

accomplishment that perhaps I had made a difference by going to Washington and speaking up. Perhaps, as Alan said, others will be saved. I believe that would make Matthew very proud and that was all the recognition I would ever need.

The wake was very touching and there were many kind words and funny stories shared about Leo and his life, which is exactly as a wake should be. A life should be remembered and celebrated with both tears and laughter. All the people who attended were warm and welcoming to me. Thanks to Charlotte's generosity, I had several appropriate dresses to choose from and never felt out of place. I was grateful, though, when everyone was gone so I could finally get a few minutes to talk with Charlotte about the Lieutenant's proposal.

"Well, that is quite a turn of events isn't it," said Charlotte thoughtfully.

"Yes indeed," I replied with a sigh.

"The fact that you did not answer him right away tells me that you really wanted to say no but didn't want to hurt his feelings."

"Honestly Charlotte, I was not sure what I wanted to say. When I married Matthew, it was because I loved him, but I was young and didn't yet understand that marriages were often more than that. They were about survival, comfort, and security. Look at Mariah. Did she love John Parker? Quite possibly she thought she did, but I think more than that she saw in him the opportunity to live a different life, a more opulent life than the one she would have with Jeremiah on the farm."

"The issue you have with her is not that she decided to secure her future. It's that she has done it with unsavory and illicit income," said Charlotte.

"Yes, I suppose that is true," I acknowledged.

"Mariah's decision is one I very much understand."

I looked at her with surprise. What was she saying? Was this about her marriage to Leo, implying that it was one driven by his wealth?

"I know what you are thinking, and it is not completely wrong, at least not now. But at the beginning, it would have been an accurate representation of our relationship. Leo wanted to marry me because he believed I would be the kind of wife he needed. I was someone who would be able to entertain important people he was trying to do business with, someone who was pleasant to look at so that other men would envy him, and lastly, someone to give him children, his legacy. I was from a respected family, but we were not well-to-do. When my father died unexpectedly, I saw in my mother the real fear that comes with limited means. I never wanted to feel that. So, I married him. That enabled me to save my mother, my sister, and myself."

"But Charlotte, I've seen how you talked about Leo. It is clear to me that you had genuine affection for him," I said, more of a question than a statement.

"It's true, I learned to love Leo. He was kind and thoughtful and he was stalwart when we lost the children. Our son died when he was only two and our daughter when she was just a year old. I had two other babies who survived less than a day, and yet each time he shared my grief and did nothing to make me feel any guilt. We became friends, we shared similar interests, and our lives complemented each other. He was generous with my mother and with Deborah's care. I will miss him profoundly and I loved him dearly."

"So, you are saying I could learn to love Richard, even though I do not now?" I asked.

"Yes. I am saying there is no shame in making a decision that makes your life and your children's lives easier and better. Whether you love him now or not, you will most certainly learn to do so. You could also have more children with him. I am sure he would embrace that, being a man of his age."

"Do you ever think about what your life might have been like if you hadn't married Leo?" I asked.

"No. I have learned I should think only about the present.

A wise man said to me once that the past and the future exist only in your mind and the only thing that is real is the present. I have tried to live by that axiom," said Charlotte as she bid me goodnight.

That night as I lay in this beautiful house, I thought about what Charlotte had said. I could not know what lay ahead, and I could not change the time already gone. A life with Richard might very well be a life well lived, but more importantly, it was here, it was now, and the chance for that kind of life might never come again. The next morning, Mrs. O'Connell helped me to pack up some of Deborah's things to take home with me. The others I would leave here as this house is likely the only place I would have to wear some of the finer dresses.

"Charlotte, I will keep you in my prayers. Please do come and see me in the city when you can, and I promise I will come to see you as often as I can," I said as I hugged her goodbye.

"Have you made a decision?" she asked.

"I have," I said smiling at her.

"Here, let me help you put that in the wagon," said Edward as he took my bag.

He waited to help me up, but even after I was seated, he hesitated. He turned to look and see if Charlotte had gone into the house, which she had.

"Millicent, I do not want you to think I have done something unsavory, but I could not help but overhear your conversation with Mrs. Whitsitt yesterday regarding your proposal from this Lieutenant and I wanted to say…" he hesitated.

"What is it, Edward? You can speak freely," I replied.

"Don't marry him, Millicent. Marry me."

Chapter Fourteen -*Begin Again*

It has been nearly three months since Leo passed away and so much has transpired since then. I never imagined that I would marry again, let alone two proposals to consider. I knew no matter which decision I made that one man would be disappointed… heartbroken even. But I thought carefully about what Charlotte had said, about the value of security, not just for myself but also for my children. She was right, of course. I have so many limitations on my own ability to provide for my family, and it nearly leaves me no choice but to marry. I also knew having once married for love, that despite the advantages, I could never marry only for financial considerations.

After an engagement of just six weeks, Edward and I were married in the parlor at Charlotte's home with her blessing. I had felt fondly toward him for some time, really since he took me to confront John Parker, but as I always hoped that Matthew would return, they were fond feelings for a friend and nothing more. But it is clear to me now that this is a marriage based on love and respect, born from friendship. It is the very best kind of marriage to have. The ceremony was a lovely affair and perfect in every way. I was sad that Kenneth was not there, but I hope when he comes home in a month or so, he will be very pleased. Charles could barely contain his excitement. Edward's brother, Mason, and Charlotte stood with us as we said our vows. I had never seen Edward smile so much. I was smiling too.

Charlotte has sold the house and returned to the city which makes me sad. I have come to love her house and more importantly, the people in it. Edward and I will see her whenever we go to visit Rebecca but that will not be as often as we could see her here. He has been given a generous pension and once we were married, he moved into the house I bought last year. We have added another bedroom and enlarged the kitchen. Edward has even built a larger barn to hold a second horse and a carriage, not just the wagon, which will be very welcome. It also meant that Charles could get another lamb which made him very excited. Lieutenant Wilson took the declining of his proposal as any gentleman would. I made a point of introducing him to Susan and last I heard they are now engaged, which makes me very happy.

The Presidential election was two weeks before the wedding and it seems impossible that the last Presidential election was four years ago when Matthew was here with me. Now I am married to someone else, living in the city. My, what change there has been. During this election, Lincoln ran with Andrew Johnson, a Southern Democrat who was intended to appeal to a broader swath of the country. Johnson made quite a name for himself at the beginning of the secession crisis when he remained in the Senate even after Tennessee seceded. This made him a hero in the North but a traitor in the eyes of many in the South. But to make the point that the Republican party was a party for all those loyal to the Union, they nominated this Southerner and Democrat for Vice President.

Lincoln and Johnson won by a landslide over General McClellan even though the war was still ongoing which many thought would be a detriment for Lincoln. Union General Sherman has been on the march headed to Georgia and there is optimism that there might be a conclusion to hostilities soon. There has been heavy fighting in Tennessee and the Union prevails now far more often than they are routed. Prisoner exchanges have begun again although too late to save my late husband. There were so many faces no longer gathered for the holidays, but it was especially sad to have Christmas without Kenneth. I am anxious to see him and to have him home with me again.

"Do you think he will have learned from this experience?" asked Edward as we sat enjoying the fire, Charles tucked into his bed.

"It is hard to say as I don't really understand how he could have committed this heinous act in the first place. What would possess the boy to do such a thing? And the bracelet? We certainly did not bring him up to be a thief."

"No, I am sure you did not, but sometimes young boys are impatient, they want the things the future brings now. They try to find a way to make those things come faster," replied Edward as he sipped his tea.

"He has been through much in his young life, and I suppose I can understand his impatience when he has seen some of the lives around him being cut short at a young age. I'm sure what Mariah did was influential too. Despite my efforts to hide that from the children, living here in town has made that impossible," I said with an air of resignation.

"Would you rather live somewhere else? We can move after Kenneth comes home, to anywhere you might want to go. Mason lives near the University of Michigan in Ann Arbor where he works; we could go there. His wife Patricia is a lovely person, and they have two boys. James is about Charles' age I think, and Oliver is about twelve. Cousins might be a welcome addition to the family," said Edward thoughtfully.

"I think that might be a very good idea if it is something to which you are open. It would be no farther to visit

Rebecca or Charlotte and it would be good to be near family," I said agreeably.

"And Mariah, there are two grandchildren now as I understand it. You would be alright with moving farther from them?"

"I would be. Mariah has her own life, which does not include me, and I do not see that changing. I never even heard from her in response to my letter that her father had died."

"I am sorry, my dear, that your relationship with her is not a better one. I support your convictions as to the source of their livelihood. We all make choices in our lives and we all must live with the consequences of those choices, both good and bad. More tea?" he said as he headed into the kitchen.

"Yes, please. Mariah may not see her lack of relationship with us as a consequence, but it is a penalty she inflicts on her brothers too, not just me," I replied somewhat angrily.

Edward kissed the top of my head as he sat my tea on the table next to me. I felt so very lucky to have him in my life at that moment. His thoughtfulness and care were so needed.

"You know, once Kenneth and Charles are a bit older, they may choose to have a relationship with her even if you do not. Moving away might deprive them of that, which may be good or bad, depending on your perspective," he said pulling his chair just a bit closer to the fire.

"I will not dictate to my children what they can and cannot do as it relates to their sister, niece, and nephew. They must decide for themselves if they are comfortable with the life their sister leads."

"Admirable of you Millie. Not everyone would be so generous, but that is just one of the many things I love about you," he murmured as he reached over and squeezed my hand.

"I love you too," I said smiling.

"You have made me very happy," said Edward.

"I could make you happier," I replied.

"No, I don't think you could, Darling. I must already be the happiest man on earth."

"Would you be happier if we had a child?" I asked with a sly smile.

"Millicent…"

"Yes, I am with child Edward."

He jumped out of his chair nearly spilling the entire contents of the table as the teacups rattled in their saucers, and he held me so tight I could barely speak.

"So, are you happier now?" I squeaked out.

"Oh my, I didn't hurt you, did I? The baby! I'm sorry, I

didn't realize I was squeezing you so tightly!"

"No, you didn't hurt me. We are both fine, my beloved," I said as I stroked his cheek.

"In this lifetime I never thought I would be a husband, that I would find someone like you, and I certainly never thought I would get a chance to be a father. I am a father to Charles and Kenneth, make no mistake, but a father to a child of my own making. You have indeed found a way to make me happier and I will spend my life, whether it be short or long, doing my very best to make you as happy as I am at this moment," he said as kissed me deeply.

We told Charles at breakfast the next morning.

"Mama, if the baby is a boy can we name it Harold?' asked Charles over bacon and eggs.

"Harold, well that's a fine name," said Edward as he smiled at Charles.

"You would want to name your brother after your best friend?" I asked.

"Yes, Harold is a very good friend to me. I heard his father once say it was a fine name. So, it would be good for my brother or sister," he replied very confidently. I could not help but laugh and Charles joined in even though I'm sure he didn't understand why I was laughing.

"I am not sure that Harold would be appropriate if the

baby is a girl," I said as I patted my not-yet-obvious belly.

"Oh, I am sure that Harold is not," added Edward laughing.

"So, what will we name the baby if it's a girl?" asked Charles.

"Well, we don't know. Do you have any ideas?" I asked.

"I still think that Harold would be good, or we could name her after you, Mama," he said with a big smile as he shoved a spoonful of eggs into his mouth.

I never imagined I would have another child and I do hope it is a girl. I miss Mariah, Rebecca, and Cordelia and while one child never replaces the loss of another, it would be good to have another girl in the house. Edward seems to have no preference. He is just thrilled to be a father after all these years. He is a wonderful husband, thoughtful, kind, attentive, and supportive. He is also already a true father to Charles. On his own accord, my son started calling him Papa Edward, which warms my heart. I'm sure *Edward* will fall by the wayside as time goes by. A letter to Kenneth telling him about our marriage went unanswered. I have only received one letter from him this entire time. I know he may feel that it is too soon as his father died just ten months ago, but he has been gone from our home for over three years. That is a long time to be alone without the love and support of a spouse.

My work at the hospital continues, but now because I enjoy it, rather than for the benefit it provides. Each morning I look forward to comforting the new patients... the scared, the sick, the dying. It is my honor to serve these men and I will continue to do it as long as they allow me to. Right now, I can hide my growing belly beneath my skirt, but it will not be long before I will have to let the waist out in my dresses and change to another style. No matter. I will do the work for as long as I can.

Today, my thoughts are not of myself. They are of the country. Word reached us this morning that President Abraham Lincoln was murdered last night while attending a play at Ford's Theater. As if in an unbelievable twist of fate, it is also the day that Union troops reoccupy Fort Sumter in South Carolina, which is the place where the war began. There is a massive manhunt underway for the assassins and Andrew Johnson has been sworn in as President. The sadness is nearly palpable, and all the storefronts are draped in black. People speak in hushed tones. You see women, and even some men, crying wherever you go. Matthew would be devastated. He had such respect and admiration for him and such high hopes for his presidency. He would have been thrilled to see him elected for a second term, but instead, he was murdered before it could even begin. Everything will be closed on the day of the funeral, except for the churches, where we will all gather to pray for his soul and our country.

The newspapers have been full of nothing but the news of the assassination and the capture of John Wilkes Booth for several weeks but now there is something else. After weeks of mourning, the country now has something to celebrate. The war is coming to an end.

General Johnston surrendered the Confederate Army of Tennessee, while General Taylor surrendered for Mississippi, Alabama, and East Louisiana. Just a few days ago, the so-called President Jefferson Davis was captured in Georgia. Lincoln did not live to see the end of the war but surely, he must have known that the end was near and that the Union would be victorious. We will be one country again, at least on paper. I fear the wounds from this division, all the pain and suffering from it, will not be forgotten for a very long time. It will take generations before men and women stop talking at their kitchen tables about the war and the price they paid, regardless of whether they were on the winning or losing side.

The spring has given way to the warmer days of summer and the day Kenneth will come home is finally here. The constable came by the house a few days ago to let me know he was being released and that he would be on one of the trains coming through today. I was so anxious I decided to simply wait at the train station all day until he arrived. I've always thought train stations and docks were interesting places. I would sit and imagine the places that people were going to, and what they were going to do there, making up stories in my mind about who they were. Spies, or doctors, or rich widows, or anything I wanted them to be.

Only one train has come in the last two hours, but the station master says there are two more trains scheduled for this afternoon. I brought a lunch and I sat quietly in the shade enjoying the day and trying to tamp down my excitement. There is another woman here waiting and she has also been here all day. She seems every bit as nervous as I am, pacing back and forth along the platform, stopping only to look down the track for any sign of a train. Finally, after another hour, her ministrations were rewarded.

I stand to get a better look at the passengers getting off the train as I glance from face to face. Young men, old men, and a few women disembark. Next come a few soldiers, one of which is destined for the nervous woman. She seemed very happy to see him. But no Kenneth. There is just one more train now, so at least I know he will be on it, and I can relax a bit knowing it will come in its own time.

"Ma'am the last train is coming," said the station master

as he gently woke me from an unexpected slumber.

"Oh, thank you very much," I said as I straightened my hat.

The train crept into the station at a snail's pace, and I could feel my nerves on edge again. Two old men, an old man with a small child, two women, another woman, a young man, and another young man poured from the train. I waited. Three men with a woman wandered off looking lost, and that was it. No more people were getting off the train today.

As I drove the carriage home, I didn't know what to think. Perhaps it was just as simple as the constable getting the day wrong. I'll ask Edward to go and see him tomorrow. For now, I am tired and hungry. I need to go home.

After Edward walked Charles to school, he headed to the constable's office as I set about doing some baking, but I found myself glancing out the window for him every few minutes. It seemed like an eternity before he returned. I went out to the barn as I could wait no longer. Moon was happy to see me as was Rosie, the mare Edward bought after we were wed.

"I would have come to you," said Edward as he was taking off Moon's tack.

"I know, but I couldn't wait. What did the Constable say? Is Kenneth coming on another day?"

"Come. Let's talk in the house," he said as he closed the stall door behind Moon before hooking up her feed bucket.

"Edward, I have dealt with much bad news in my life, and I can hear it here as well as in the house. Now what did he say?" I said with exasperation.

"I'm sorry, of course you have. I sometimes forget how strong you are. Kenneth was released yesterday. The boys are given a knapsack with their clothes, a sandwich, and enough money to purchase a train ticket when they are dropped at the station. The constable confirmed via telegraph that Kenneth was dropped there with several other boys but apparently, he did not buy a ticket or bought a ticket to another destination."

"Edward, what are you saying? Kenneth is not coming home?"

"I'm saying we don't know if he will come home or not. It may simply be that he wants some time on his own before he does," said Edward optimistically.

"Why would he do such a thing? He's just a boy, only sixteen."

"He's a young man Millie. He's working and men his age are doing all kinds of things. Let's just give it a few days and see. I don't think there is any reason to think that he is in danger or that something untoward has befallen him. I'm sorry. I know you are disappointed, but he must follow his own mind and heart," he said as he held me close to him.

The days turned into weeks. I finally stopped thinking that he might return. For whatever reason he has decided to go his own way, perhaps from the shame of what he did, or maybe just to get a new start somewhere else. All I could do now was to pray for his health and safety and hope that wherever life takes him he is happy. Charles is crushed I'm sure, but he says nothing of it. My heart just breaks for this boy. His birthday is a subdued affair. Edward took him fishing which cheered him up, but not as much as fishing with his brother would have.

"Charles, we've decided to go ahead and put the baby in the new room, so you can have a room to yourself. Isn't that wonderful? You wanted your own room when we came here and now you will have it."

"I'd rather have Kenneth back than my own room mama," he said mournfully.

"Of course you would. I would too, but whether or not Kenneth returns to us is his decision and one we must respect, even if we don't want to," I said as I hugged him close to me.

"Mama I can feel the baby kicking!" he said excitedly putting his hand on my now very rotund belly.

"Yes, the baby is getting very close now. Just a few more

weeks. I'm going to need you to help us get the room ready," said Edward, smiling at him.

"I can do that, but first I have to feed Daisy," he said as he ran out the back door.

Edward and I couldn't help but laugh. The room was a few weeks off but his new lamb, Daisy, certainly wouldn't want to wait on her food.

A letter came today from Kenneth for which I was very grateful. At least now I knew he was alive and well. Maybe even happy.

Mama,

I'm sorry it has taken me so long to write, but I wanted to wait until I was settled in a place where you could write me back. I know I have worried you, but I did not mean to do so. In reform school, I learned a lot about myself and why I did what I did, although I'm not still sure that I can explain it in words. While I was there, I met another boy. His name is Adam Beren, and his family has a large horse ranch in a place called Kalamazoo. He was released one day after me, and he invited me to come and work on his parent's ranch, knowing they were always in need of good hands. I have been here now for some time, and I am very happy. We work hard every day. There are four of us, and we live together in a bunkhouse. It's kind of like having a bunch of older brothers, which you can imagine has both good and bad parts. I do miss Charles, though, so please tell him I said hello.

For now, I will stay here, but I may come home at some point. You can write to me, and I promise I will write you back more quickly than before. I did get your letter that you and Mr. Fuller have married. I am happy for you. I know he will be a good father to Charles.

Your loving son,
Kenneth

I carefully folded up his letter and put it in the small box where I kept all the letters from Matthew. It was good to know that he was doing well, thriving even. Despite missing him, I am indeed happy for him.

The baby's room is ready. Charles helped Edward paint the nursery a pale yellow. They also made a bassinet and a rocker. I am ready now, more than ready. It is difficult to walk now as the baby is so heavy and low. The midwife is coming to check on me every day and she is sure it will not be more than a couple of days. It is difficult to sleep and during the night my thoughts often turn to the children I have given birth to that are no longer with me. This baby seems strong, and I am hopeful, but I know nothing is a given. God makes all the decisions in this regard, and we can only accept them. As I lay here watching Edward sleeping, I also wonder what

Matthew would think of the turn my life has taken. He met Edward, I seem to recall, but I have no recollection of anything he might have said about it. The moon is bright making it difficult to see the lights from the lighthouse reflecting on the ceiling. I have come to love those lights, always there for me night after night, during my loneliest hours. As I was just about to fall asleep, I was jolted awake by a pain I immediately recognized.

"Edward," I said as I shook him gently.

"Millie are you alright?" he said, rubbing the sleep from his eyes as he tried to sit up.

"Yes, but my labor has started. It will be quick I'm sure as Charles came in less than an hour. I think it would be best if you got the midwife," I said calmly.

"I'll be right back," he said jumping up out of bed, quickly pulling on his pants and throwing on a sweater before bolting out the bedroom door.

I lay back on the bed for a moment as another pain began. Everything we would need was already gathered in the basket next to the bed. The pressure in my loins was building and I knew the baby was indeed going to come quickly. Hopefully, Edward would make it back in time. I'd done without a midwife before, but I had Matthew with me. Charles is too young to be of any help. I've never done this alone. Before I could begin to panic, Edward came crashing through the door again the midwife in tow.

"Ah, Mrs. Fuller! I see things are progressing quickly," she said as she peeked underneath the sheet.

"Yes indeed," I said, in between pains.

"Step outside Mr. Fuller. I will get you when the women have done their work," said Mrs. Halle as she showed him the door.

"I love you, Darling. I will be right outside," he said, clearly nervous.

"All right, Mrs. Fuller. Let's get this child born," she said as she plopped the birth basket on the bed.

The sun was just barely peeking up over the horizon, a thin band of pink and gold, when Mrs. Halle handed me my precious bundle, red in the face from crying.

"Mr. Fuller, it is done. You can come in now," said Mrs. Halle, "Congratulations," she said as she brushed passed him.

"Hello," he said as he sat down on the side of the bed, pushing the hair from my face. "How are you?"

"I am wonderful. Would you like to meet your daughter?" I asked as I pulled back the blanket.

"Goodness, Millie. What a splendid child she is, just like her mother!" he said as he kissed me on the cheek, grinning from ear to ear.

"She is, isn't she?" I whispered as I handed her to him.

He held her in his arms as if she were made of fine china and it made me smile. He would get more comfortable in a few weeks, but for now, it was so endearing to see him behave in this way.

"What shall we call her Millie?"

"I was thinking we could call her Charlotte Cordelia Fuller. What do you think?" I asked as I took her back from him and put her on my breast.

"I think that would be perfect. We can call her Lottie," he said as he kissed me.

Charles was disappointed we didn't name her Harold. I think he was also a bit disappointed the baby wasn't a boy, but perhaps there would be another. We will see. Edward was incredibly helpful while I was recovering from the birth by cooking and looking after Charles. Those first few days were blissful and calm. Lottie was strong with her feeding and cried very little and so it was a blessing to have this time with her.

"Mama, can I come in?" said Charles, peeking through the door.

"Of course, come here climb up next to me," I said, patting the bed.

"Is she sleeping?" he asked.

"Yes, she just finished eating. Now she's taking a nap. That's mostly what babies do when they are first born."

"Did I do that?" he asked skeptically.

"You certainly did. Sleep and eat, then sleep and eat."

"I still do that," he said with a giggle.

"Yes, you do," I replied, smiling at him softly.

"Lottie, it's me. Your big brother Charles," he whispered in her ear. "I'm here to look after you and keep you safe because that's what big brothers do."

Chapter Fifteen - *To Say Your Name*

"Charles, slow down! Lottie can't walk that fast," I called out.

"Sorry Mama. Come here, Lottie. Let me hold your hand," he said as he ran back to her.

"I'm going as fast I can," she exclaimed.

The first day of school is always so exciting. Lottie's first year, and Charles' last. I watched from the porch as they walked down the street together, Charles stopping to collect his friends along the way. I shifted Caleb to my other hip. My goodness, he's getting big.

"Wave bye-bye," I said to which he quickly obliged, and he even got out a respectable version of the words.

"Here, let me take him," said Edward as he came out onto the porch.

We sat at the table finishing our tea and reading through the paper, Caleb having gone done for a nap.

"Millie, did you see this article about Andersonville?"

Just hearing that name always gives me a chill. After the war, even more stories of the horrors there were revealed. The men who survived were so severely emaciated and diseased that many of them have died over the last few years as a direct result of their treatment there. Thirteen thousand men died there. At its worst, three thousand men died in a single day.

"No, I did not read it. What does it say?"

"A man named Dorance Atwater was a Union soldier who worked as a clerk at the camp. He kept records of all the men who died there and the number of their locations. Clara Barton joined him last year in trying to identify more of the soldiers buried there. Now they are having a ceremony to consecrate the ground and to form a National Cemetery honoring those who died there," he said as he lowered the paper.

My heart skipped a beat. I had always assumed that Matthew was buried in an unmarked location which would never be known. Is it possible that his burial site is marked?

"So, are you saying that they know where Matthew is buried and that we could go there?" I asked with some trepidation.

"I believe the answer to both of those things is yes. I would suggest we write to them at this Missing Soldiers office in Washington and see if they do in fact know the location of Matthew's burial."

"If they do, would you be open to traveling there? To visit the gravesite... " I said as my voice trailed off.

Edward came around the table and knelt next to me, taking both my hands in his.

"Of course, I would. If that is what you would like to do, by all means, we can arrange it. I can see in your eyes how very important to you that might be," he said sincerely.

"I always felt that Matthew's departure from this world was left undone in some way. No burial, no words to commemorate his life, no place for me to go and say my piece to him. It all seemed very harsh in my mind," I said sadly.

"Let me write to them and see what I can find out. Would you let me do that for you?"

"Thank you, Darling. Thank you," I said as I kissed him.

It was nearly two months before we received a reply. Honestly, I was not sure that I expected to hear anything at all. What they had to say surprised me.

May 12, 1870

Missing Soldiers Office

Dear Mrs. Fuller,

First, let me say we honor the sacrifice of Sergeant Matthew Wagner, and we also recognize the pain and suffering of his family. Through the work we have done reviewing records seized after the war as well as records kept by Mr. Atwater, we have identified the gravesite of your deceased loved one. If you would like to visit the cemetery, we would be happy to welcome you and show you where Sargent Wagner is interred.

There is also a plan underway to provide headstones for all the graves but as you can imagine that will take some time. Each stone will contain the name of the soldier, the state from which they enlisted, the year of their death, and the number of the gravesite. Burials are in numerical order which facilitates locating any grave in the vast cemetery.

Again, my sincerest condolences on your loss.

Regards,

Miss Lois Brown

Assistant to Mr. Atwater

I sat looking at the letter for some time, very much as I had with the letters I received from Matthew years ago. Did I want to go and visit his grave? Or did I want to just put it behind me knowing now that he will be accounted for in annals of history? Edward was very kind about the whole thing, and I knew he would do whatever I wished to do. I wondered if I should talk to Charles about what we have learned and if he would want to go. As a boy of fifteen now, he barely remembers his father. As I had thought, he now refers to Edward as Papa. Would it be worse for him to relive this sadness?

Several weeks passed before I broached the subject with him and while he appreciated knowing where his father was buried, he felt no need to visit. I, on the other hand, decided that Edward and I would go. His sister-in-law agreed to come and stay with the children while we traveled. I thought about taking Caleb with us, but it will be a long journey by train and carriage. We will also stop to see Rebecca on our way home and children are not allowed there.

As the day of our departure arrived my emotions were a jumble of anticipation and fear. What would it feel like to stand among the horror that was Andersonville? So much suffering and pain had occurred there, it must have scarred the land and the very air of that place. I was sure you could not go there without feeling it. We would need to take two trains to get there, and it would be a full two-day journey. Edward had arranged for a Pullman sleeper for the part of our journey that would be overnight which was very much appreciated. When Charlotte and I traveled to Washington we sat up all night, which was exhausting.

Once we arrive in Americus, Georgia we will have to take a carriage as soon as we arrive to return to town and our hotel before dark. There was no place to stay closer to our destination so our time there would be somewhat limited.

"Are you ready, my dear?" said Edward after we said our

goodbyes to the children and our thanks to Patricia for staying with them.

"Yes, I am ready," I replied as I followed him out to the carriage waiting to take us to the train station.

The last time I had been on this platform was to wait for Kenneth's return. It seemed like a very long time ago. We thought about moving away, and perhaps we still will when Charles finishes his schooling, but this place feels so much like my home now that it's hard to think of leaving it.

"Let me help you ma'am," said the station master as he took my hand to steady my ascent up the stairs into the train car.

"Thank you, sir," said Edward as he returned from dropping our bags to receive me at the top of the stairs.

I stopped and turned to look at the station master standing there on the platform. He was older and grayer, of course, but I realized it was the same man who had been here the day I waited for Kenneth. He seemed to remember me too as he smiled and tipped his hat to me. Edward led me down the corridor to our private room which was nicely appointed. There was a Hooper toilet and a small sink in the toilet room next door. I settled in next to the window with Edward sitting across from me.

We said little during the trip to Washington, where we

would change trains. Edward read the paper as I watched as the landscape changed, undulating up and down… flat, then hilly. Cities and farmland alternated in shades of gray, then green, then gray again. People, cows, horses, each in their place, the cities bustling with wagons and carriages, everyone hurrying to go one place or another. Little farms dotted the land with barns of red and houses of white. Could it be only five years ago that men were fighting and dying on this very land? It all seemed so normal and serene now.

"Millie, we are pulling into the station," said Edward which startled me from a deep sleep.

"Oh goodness, I didn't intend to sleep," I said as smoothed my dress and looked out the window.

Washington had changed quite a bit since I was here last. The station was a different one now and it was much larger and grander than before. There were throngs of people and I held tightly onto Edward's arm so we would not become separated. A porter helped to gather our small bags and transfer them to the other train which was just a few lines over. There were at least six or seven different rail lines in this station alone. I had never seen anything like it, and I was relieved when we boarded our next train. Once safely in our berth, I was able to watch the hustle and bustle outside the window without feeling pummeled by it. It would be about half an hour before our train departed and Edward went to get a newspaper from the stand on the platform. His absence made me nervous, and I fretted the whole time that he might not make it back before the train departed, but at last, the door slid open.

"See, I told you I would make it back in time," he said as he kissed me on the cheek.

"Yes, I know you did, but you know I have moments where I cannot control my own anxiety, and this was one of those."

"I am sorry I made you anxious. I did not mean to. I was able to get two newspapers and a chocolate bar to share later. As soon as we depart we can go to the dining car for supper if you would like."

"That would be wonderful. It amazes me that they can cook and serve meals on the train all while it's moving," I replied.

"It is indeed. I remember traveling with Leo and Charlotte and having to pack a large hamper of food and drink. You could not buy anything at the station except tickets. The world is changing Millie. I cannot even begin to imagine how things will be for our grandchildren," he said with a sigh.

"Better, I hope. Not just different, but better," I replied.

Dinner was wonderful and for a change, we indulged in some wine which was also very good. When we returned to our berth the seats had been turned into a bed that was made up with sheets, blankets, and pillows. It was cramped, but we managed to change into our night clothes, and I climbed in first next to the window. Edward thought it would be safer this way in case someone should try to come into the berth during the night. We sat up for a bit reading the paper but once the sun had set, I was ready to sleep. Edward was still reading when I turned over and closed my eyes.

I slept surprisingly well, perhaps due to the constant motion and noise of the train. I hadn't even been aware of the stops we made during the night. When I stepped off the train it was obvious that we were no longer in Michigan. The air was humid and hot even though summer had barely just begun, and the sun wasn't even fully up yet. I was wishing I had worn a lighter dress. Edward deftly loaded our things in the carriage he had arranged for us, and we set off to the cemetery.

Once out of town, the landscape was simply forest and farms with trees lining the well-maintained road. There were several other wagons and carriages that also seemed to be heading that way and we traveled along in a bit of a caravan for many miles. One of the wagons peeled off right before we arrived but the others continued until we reached a large wrought iron gate. The gate was open and there was a small farmhouse just inside where we stopped to get directions. There were many people gathered there for the consecration ceremony that would take place later in the morning. We followed the hand-drawn map the man had provided until we found the burial grounds. It was not what I had expected. There were young pecan trees that had been planted throughout the property and the open space was surrounded by beautiful mature trees. In one area, some men were building a monument of some sort on behalf of the State of New York to memorialize their dead. There were small round markers at each grave, but you could already see a few of the headstones Miss Brown had mentioned being installed. Edward and I walked along this so-called Section H, checking the numbers at the end of each of the rows.

"Here, Millie. I think it would be this row," he said, stopping at one of the rows two ahead of me on the left.

I could feel my heart starting to race a bit so close now to where Matthew was buried.

"Would you like to go the rest of the way by yourself?"

"Yes, I think I would. Thank you, Dearest," I said.

There were a few other people in the cemetery also looking for the graves of their loved ones, but they were not near us. We were now only a few rows from the back, the forest not being far away. I could hear the birds singing and calling to each other from the trees as I walked down the row, the markers getting closer and closer to the one I was searching for. 11756,11755, 11754… and then in front of me was 11753. I stood for a moment looking at the small round marker at my feet. He was here, beneath me. I knelt on the grass and removed my hat. The breeze was thankfully cool and light, the sun just reaching the tops of the trees, filtering through the branches and leaves to the east of where I sat. Edward remained at the end of the row, quietly waiting with his head bowed, perhaps in prayer for these men who had their lives cut short.

"Matthew, it's me, Millicent," I said quietly as I ran my fingers through the blades of grass. "I know you have waited a long time for someone to come and say your name, but I am here. I'm sure you found Cordelia and Dickie when you arrived. I'm sorry I did not tell you about her death before, but I thought it more than you could bear. The other children are well. Mariah, Rebecca, Kenneth, and Charles. Oh, and you have grandchildren! Mariah has both a son and a daughter and Kenneth has just married so there will be more soon. I have married again, as I hope you would have wanted, and I have two more children with Edward. He is a good father to

Charles, and we are lucky to have him."

My heart was so full, and I wasn't sure what I wanted to say… what I needed to say. I had thought about this moment many times, more than I could count to be sure. I sighed as I began again.

"I want you to know that I tried. I tried my very best to save you. I'm sorry I was not able to do so. The Union won, Matthew. We are united again and slavery has been abolished across the land. The future that you gave your life for came to be. I wish you were here to see it. You would be so happy. We do our very best to keep your memory alive. My youngest son is even named in your honor. His name is Caleb Matthew Fuller. You might remember that my mother always used to say that if you say someone's name and remember them fondly, they are not really gone. It was something her grandmother used to say. I know you are not here, not really, but I hope from heaven you can hear us when we speak of you. The one place you have never been gone from is my heart. You are there, my Darling, as you always were, and always shall be."

I picked a small white flower growing in the grass and laid it on the white disk with the number of his grave. I breathed in the air. For the first time in a very long time, my heart was still. I was no longer anxious or afraid. I heard a large bird cry out and I shielded my eyes from the rising sun as I looked for it in the sky. I did not see him, not at first. But then, it cried out again and I was able to see it. A hawk was sitting on a limb of one of the pecan trees. He looked at me cocking his head back and forth as if he was studying me. The natives believed hawks were the souls of our loved ones coming to reassure us. I had heard my grandmother telling my mother about it not long before she died. Suddenly, the hawk took flight, swirling and swirling up into the sky until I lost sight. I sat a bit longer before finally rising, brushing the grass off my dress, as Edward appeared at my side.

"Millicent are you alright?" he asked with a note of concern.

"I am," I said smiling at him. "It's an oddly beautiful place, isn't it? So peaceful and serene. It is not at all the place I thought it would be... although the sheer number of dead here does take one's breath away."

"Indeed. It is beautiful in a melancholy kind of way, but you are right. The enormity of what happened here cannot be understated. Are you ready to go to the ceremony now, my Dear?" he asked.

"Yes, I am. Truly ready."

Author's Note

Andersonville National Historic Site began as a stockade built about 18 months before the end of the U.S. Civil War to hold Union Army prisoners captured by Confederate soldiers. Located deep behind Confederate lines, the 26.5-acre Camp Sumter (named for the South Georgia county it occupied) was designed for a maximum of 10,000 prisoners. At its most crowded, it held more than 32,000 men, many of them wounded and starving, in horrific conditions with rampant disease, contaminated water, and only minimal shelter from the blazing sun and the chilling winter rain. In the prison's 14 months of existence, some 45,000 Union prisoners arrived here; of those, 12,920 died and were buried in a cemetery created just outside the prison walls.

The cemetery site serving Camp Sumter was established as Andersonville National Cemetery on July 26, 1865. By 1868, the cemetery held the remains of more than 13,800 Union soldiers whose bodies had been retrieved after their deaths in hospitals, battles, or prison camps throughout the region. Andersonville National Cemetery has been used continuously since its founding and currently averages over 150 burials a year. The cemetery and associated prison site became a unit of the National Park System in 1970.

Today, Andersonville National Historic Site comprises three distinct components: the former site of <u>Camp Sumter military prison</u>, the <u>Andersonville National Cemetery</u>, and the <u>National Prisoner of War Museum</u>, which opened in 1998 to honor all U.S. prisoners of war in all wars.

On its worst day, nearly 3,000 people died. My great-great-great grandfather, Shubal Dutton, was one of those. He is grave 11753. This story was inspired by his life and legacy. If you visit the park, which I highly encourage, please stop by and pay your respects.